THE
PLUPERFECT
OF LOVE

THE PLUPERFECT OF LOVE

DOROTHY CRAYDER

illustrated by Paulita Sedgwick

ATHENEUM

1971 NEW YORK

pluperfect *adj.* [L. *plus-quam-perfectum* (sc. *tempus* tense)] more than perfect; cf. F. *plus-que-parfait*

To Robert
and our daughter, Hila

THE
PLUPERFECT
OF LOVE

CHAPTER I

THE CASTLE stood high on a rock, alone and
dark in the mauve twilight, the mauve that is the
color of gloom and magic—of elsewhere.

No one expects a castle to be quick and easy to get to,
and this one was no exception. To reach it one had
first of all to know the way, then there was the steep
winding path, and finally the long broken flight of steps.
Only someone with a good reason would be making this
climb at this hour with the wind so cold and the place
so forlorn.

Or someone with an unreasonable impulse.

As if her feet knew something she did not, Zena had
made the detour to the castle in a breathless rush. But as
she climbed the steps, the wind blew stronger, holding
her back, blowing her long yellow hair across her eyes
and blinding her. By the time she reached the stone

forecourt of the castle, she was gasping and it was a minute before she could breathe again.

In that minute could someone have fled? She had half expected someone to be waiting for her. She walked around, looking and listening. Slowly, she scanned the facade of the gray stone castle, up and down to the top of its single tower, pausing at the narrow black windows; she toured the crenelated rampart; she went to the rear of the castle where the rock dropped dangerously. No one was to be seen or heard. She was alone. There were those who would be afraid to be in this place, at this time, alone. But Zena was famous for being brave.

Here, at the castle, she was above the tree tops of the park; beyond the park, all around it, was the city. From here, one had an eagle's view; one could see far and wide and into tomorrow.

All at once, this was the reason for coming here and she moved swiftly to the south rampart. Leaning over the parapet, her eyes went past the tops of trees, past the leaves drifting from them, past the lake, past a rider disappearing in the twilight, until they found their mark.

It was a light that flared in a golden fan from a chateau-like roof silhouetted against the mauve sky. There, at the Plaza, presently there would be music, a waltz no doubt, and flowers and soft laughter, of course. So it was rumored. The Plaza was a hotel that bred legend— like Camelot.

Zena forgot the cold and the wind. A wind stronger than the one outside was suddenly blowing through her, carrying her toward that light.

4

Was it there that she would be set free and live happily ever after? She asked where there was no one to hear this embarrassing question, embarrassing, that is, to people who preferred statistics to fairy tales.

And having asked that one, there was no point in stopping: Was it there that she would meet her Own True Love?

There was no answering omen, unless it was some purple beginning to creep into the mauve, foreshadowing night. Perhaps it was this purple that now made her feel the way an echo sounded—lonely and lamenting and elsewhere-ish.

She almost wished she had not allowed herself to come here, had not tried to peer into the future like some gypsy fortune teller. After all, until now the present had done nicely, in spite of such inconveniences as being imprisoned in a house of secrets.

And yet, though it was time to go home, there was something here at the castle that still pulled like a magnet.

It was, to say the least, confusing.

With a last, lingering look at the fan of light over the Plaza, Zena left the rampart and crossed the court still half expecting to meet someone. Indeed, as she made the descent from the castle, she continued to look and to listen. But when it wasn't the wind she heard or the groaning branch of a tree or the flight of a bird, it was leaves crunching under her feet.

She walked past a garden filled with dying rue and rosemary, past a lake where ducks waited patiently for night to fall, past a squirrel heading home in an elm. With the coming of night, the park began to belong to its own.

Beyond the park, where the Plaza was to be seen through the shedding trees, the skyline of the city was lighting up. At that time, before the Empire State and various other skyscrapers had been built, the skyline of Central Park South hung low and did not get in the way of birds migrating or flights of fancy.

When Zena came out of the park on to Central Park West, everything was quite as it should be. Gentlemen who kept bankers' hours were homeward bound in chauffeur driven automobiles such as Pierce-Arrows and Stanley Steamers and Locomobiles. And elderly ladies whose horses had been retired to distant pastures were timidly driving their electric broughams at speeds of ten miles an hour. Seamstresses, ordinary house-wives, messengers, high school people, and those merely democratically inclined rode the trolley car then running on Central Park West.

On that particular late afternoon, it was an orderly procession. No one was prepared for what was about to take place. Everyone was minding his or her own business.

Except Zena. Zena enjoyed minding other people's business; it was always interesting and sometimes amusing. Although she was not particular, anyone's would do, these days it was flappers' business that was by all odds the most fascinating.

6

And just then, two flappers came down the avenue aflame with *lipstick* (forbidden to girls who were not flappers). Girls who were flappers didn't care what anyone said about them, because they wanted the whole world to know they were flappers. And they didn't care if they got round shouldered either. Slouching the way flappers should, these two walked with their shoulders hunched in the debutante slouch. And they were having a *conversation*, a deep one it would appear.

With ears twitching, Zena planned to follow close on their heels.

Oh, famous flappers (some said infamous), what do you talk *about?* Is it about the wild and wonderful ways of Flaming Youth? Of Free This and Free That and Free Love . . . ?

It was precisely at the moment when Zena was within earshot of these two flappers that it happened.

A black electric brougham making its sedate way south toward the Hotel Plaza suddenly went out of control. Without any warning, without so much as a peep of its horn, this most sedate vehicle veered east, cut across a coffee-colored Locomobile, a Pierce-Arrow landaulet, and a horse-drawn ice wagon. The chauffeurs of the Locomobile and the Pierce-Arrow cursed furiously, and the horse screamed. Even ladies shouted—those who had not fainted or were not sniffing smelling salts. One suffragist so lost her head she quite forgot women had recently won the vote and took this opportunity to demand it all over again. And the flappers forgot who they were and straightened up, rigid with fright.

Where all had been order on Central Park West, all was now chaos.

And Zena, who loved excitement more than she was afraid of being run over by a black electric, watched from the curb.

To everyone's amazement, the black electric turned out to be under perfect control and knew exactly where it was going. Slipping past a trolley car ringing its bell frantically, the electric headed for the little girl with the yellow hair and came to a stop directly in front of her.

A light was switched on in the dove-colored interior of the electric and illuminated a crystal vase holding one perfect yellow rose. To everyone's further amazement, the person at the steering bar of the electric was not a fragile little old lady, but a powerful and exquisitely dapper gentleman, vaguely middle-aged.

Lightly and gracefully for such a large man, he stepped from the brougham and took notice of the commotion he had caused. Some rubberneckers had gathered around him. With a flick of his hand, he sent them scurrying. However, it was the flappers at whom he glared. Many people glare; most to no avail. This gentleman's glare was as potent as dragon fire. The flappers tried first to show their distaste for this gentleman by glaring back, then they tried for jaunty indifference, but the gentleman's glare was too much even for them. They, too, fled, but more like rabbits fleeing a natural enemy than like the symbol of the brave new world.

Only Zena, who was famous for her bravery, stood her ground. The gentleman stared down at her. He

8

lifted his black fedora and uncovered hair the color of the devil's own red.

"Ah . . . yes, yes," he said with his eyes fastened on Zena. "Ah . . . my dear little girl, have you by any chance seen ah . . . seen a cat, a black one with ah . . . with yellow eyes?"

Zena, something of an expert, suspected this gentleman of fibbing, of pretending to have lost a cat.

"Did you say yellow?"

"Yellow as a rose is yellow."

The gentleman's fire not having been directed at the automobiles or the trolley car, they had not moved and their passengers were either frankly or surreptitiously gawking.

"Sir, hadn't you better tell them you're just looking for a cat?" Zena suggested.

The gentleman turned and glared again as he signaled for the vehicles to move on. All did except for one Model T Ford. Not only did it not budge, but its owner got out and came toward them. He was an upstate farmer who had a long and difficult journey ahead over two lane roads, unpaved roads, and who, no doubt, would also have to contend with several flat tires. But never mind.

"Little girl, isn't this man a stranger to you?" the farmer asked.

"Of course he is," Zena replied with delight. She didn't care what anyone said; herself, she liked strangers very much.

"Of course he is not," the red-haired gentleman said,

now glaring at the farmer.

The farmer who had lived through drought, flood, hurricane, and a vile tempered bull, stood *his* ground.

"One of you has got to be wrong," he said.

"She is," said the gentleman.

"Prove it," said the farmer.

The gentleman reached into his chesterfield and brought out a gold cigarette case. The wind suddenly gusted to gale force, but this gentleman lit his cigarette on the first light and without sheltering the flame. Zena and the farmer were impressed.

Puffing on his cigarette, the gentleman spoke nonchalantly: "Birthstone sapphire, birthplace south chamber seventh floor many-gabled house yonder. To this day resides—yonder."

"What do you say, little girl?" the farmer asked.

"I'd say he's getting stranger and stranger."

"Aha! Knew it. Why don't you just get into that contraption of yours and take yourself right back where you came from before I call the police. And as for you, little girl—"

"But every word he said is the truth! So far, that is . . ."

The farmer scowled.

"Well, this is as far as I'm going. Where I come from, at dusk a little girl like you is home where she belongs helping her ma with the chores. If it was up to me, I'd give this whole blasted island right back to the Indians—"

The farmer's hat blew off, and he went flying after it.

Zena's normal impulse would have been to join him because it was fun to chase hats in a high wind and because it was polite to thank someone for trying to rescue you. But a stronger impulse held her back.

"Oh, sir, who are you, sir?" she asked the gentleman.

"Ah, I'm glad you asked that question."

Once again he reached into his chesterfield; this time it was for a leather calling card case. He handed her a parchment card. Zena, whose vision was twenty-twenty, was able to read it in the fading light:

JABEZ

Matchmaker

By appointment to
Their Majesties
The Kings and Queens of Many Realms

Zena was flabbergasted.

"A *matchmaker!* A person who finds a husband for a lady who wishes to be a wife? And vice versa? For goodness sake, is that who you are?"

He bowed. "At your service. That is, when the time comes."

"Oh! What a nice coincidence this is!"

"I beg your pardon?"

"Oh, Mr. Jabez—"

"Please!" He raised his hand. "One does not speak of *Mr.* Beethoven nor *Mr.* Shakespeare, does one? I do not wish to be immodest, but what Beethoven did for sym-

11

phony making and Shakespeare did for sonnet making, Jabez has done for matchmaking."

"That's beautiful. What a beautiful coincidence this is."

"Coincidence? You were already, at such an early age —early for this culture to be sure—considering the services of a matchmaker?"

"Frankly, I hadn't thought of a matchmaker, but—"

"But?"

She was not ready to finish that sentence. "But you can't imagine how happy I am you—uh—you lost your cat," she improvised.

"Ah yes, the cat. He will return. He always does. You call it a coincidence." His eyes narrowed as he studied her. "I call it a miracle. Yes, a miracle if ever I saw one."

Zena was too busy examining the card to give this remark her attention.

"But there isn't any address on this card. How is a person supposed to find you?"

"By following instructions."

"Yes sir?"

"Listen carefully."

Zena stepped closer to the gentleman.

"*When the time comes*, when the time comes for you to get in touch with me, you will need to light a candle. I regret to say that, childish though it may be, one still needs the candle. You will hold this card over the candle and you will spell the name Jabez. You will give each letter its proper due. *Properly* given—kindly note the emphasis on the word properly—my exceedingly private number will appear in the lower right hand corner of the card."

"What fun!"

"Fun? My dear girl, this is no laughing matter. This is deadly serious. Moreover, I must extract a promise from you. I have been careless. I who am never careless have been so because I am off schedule today, way off I might say, and—not altogether myself. I should of course have extracted the promise before I revealed my identity."

"Oh, don't worry about that. If it's important, I can keep a promise."

"But can you keep a secret?"

"A secret? Oh, dear! I did promise in blood not to keep any secrets from my best friend Vera."

"Forget Vera. It is Jabez who is your best friend."

"He is?"

"As of this minute. In a manner of speaking. But only on the condition that you keep me a secret from *everyone* which includes your nearest, your dearest, your ex-best friend, and your enemies, until further notice. Is that understood?"

"But—but why?"

"Because I say so."

Zena hoped it was only her imagination, but Jabez sounded more menacing than friendly. Nevertheless, she could not resist asking what would happen if she did not promise to keep him a secret.

"I will change my private number."

"In that case, I certainly do promise."

13

"Solemnly?"

"Very solemnly."

"A sensible decision. Now then. Take the Tootsie Roll, the aggie, and the two immies out of your right-hand coat pocket."

"For goodness sake! How ever did you know?" Zena asked as she took these objects out of her pocket.

"There is now left in the pocket the deck of Old Maid cards. Am I correct?"

"You certainly are, sir."

"Now then. While I hold the candy and the marbles, you are to slip my card into the pack of Old Maid and keep it there, hidden from the rest of the world, until the time comes. Is that clearly understood?"

"But what if I want to play Old Maid?"

"And why should you want to do that anymore? I detest that game. I detest that expression. There are no Old Maids. There are only unfortunates who do not have my assistance. Do as you are told."

Zena, who was not naturally obedient, obeyed.

"As a matter of curiosity, regarding Tootsie Rolls, don't they give you spots?"

"Nothing gives me pimples. Not even hot fudge sundaes with nuts and marshmallow whip. Not even a million charlotte russes."

"I thought as much," Jabez murmured. "I can see that with you it is all going to be different, very different."

"Is that good or bad, sir?"

"That remains to be seen." Jabez drew on his cigarette thoughtfully. "And a word remains for me to

14

speak. A word or two now, rather more later—when the time comes."

"Yes?"

"About those flappers—"

"Oh, sir, what about them?"

"It will do you no good to chase after them. And worse than no good to emulate them."

"But—oh dear, but—"

"Flappers live by false illusions."

"They do? False? I didn't know there were any other kind, sir."

"Which only goes to prove that you have much to learn—from me."

"But, sir, only the other day I saw in the dictionary that the whole meaning of illusion is that it's—"

"Never mind the dictionary. When it comes to illusions, it is Jabez who is the expert, not that Mr. Webster. It will be to your advantage to remember that."

"Oh," said Zena.

"Ah," said Jabez. "Now, as I said before, I am late . . . and I am early, altogether off schedule . . . and it is time for me to continue on my way. I do so reluctantly. This evening my way leads to the debut of a young lady with the most unfortunate habit of giggling at the wrong moment." He glared. "I will soon put a stop to that."

"How?" Zena asked, her curiosity often getting the better of her judgment.

"I ask the questions. I do not always choose to answer them."

"I didn't know that."

"Now you do." He pulled the black fedora down over one eye. "Until we meet again." He waved his hand in a gesture of farewell which unexpectedly ended with a snap of his fingers.

Too lightly, too swiftly, Jabez glided into the black electric. Just before the door closed, a large black cat with yellow eyes slid in beside him.

Transfixed, Zena stood and watched the electric disappear. Then, she floated home in the mauve twilight, floated and whirled every now and then as she waltzed.

THE SEVENTH FLOOR of the many-gabled house was very like a vast dark forest with velvets and tapestries shrouding mahogany and walnut and oak as if in a pall of Spanish moss. Seeming to come from the distant heart of this dark forest, the ticking of clocks deepened the hush. Persons entering here for the first time dropped their voices to whispers; timid persons lost their voices altogether.

Zena, entering, usually shouted. "Crystal!" she would shout and run to Crystal with something or other bubbling to be told. Crystal the cook had known Zena since the day she was born and in a house where a person who had no brothers or sisters could get lonely if she were so inclined, Zena had Crystal.

Now, having floated past doormen and elevator men and an assortment of neighbors, all of whom were startled, Zena entered still floating and, instead of shouting, she hummed softly to herself. She floated past a parlor-maid and a chambermaid and a waitress, all of whom thought she was a caution. They gaped and they gawked and they giggled.

As she floated toward the kitchen, she could not help but smile with pride at the thought that it was she who now had the biggest secret of all in this house of secrets.

The kitchen was huge, and a small figure working dough at the great marble table in its center ought to have been dwarfed. But Crystal had been preshrunk, so to speak, and was stubbornly resistant to being diminished by anything or anybody.

"And why was there no rowdy shouting today?" Crystal, preoccupied with her dough, asked dreamily.

Zena had her answer ready: "Because, darling Crystal, you always say that girls who shout today will have stringy necks tomorrow."

"And so suddenly you have decided to heed my words of wisdom?"

"I thought it would please you."

"Flattery will get you no place." Crystal stroked the dough tenderly. "You are hiding something from me. Go get yourself your nourishment and then come back and tell me what it's all about. I'll be waiting, ducky."

Ominous as that sounded, Zena was prepared for that too. She had a problem to discuss that should do very nicely to divert Crystal from the big secret she was keeping. It was a practical problem that had just surfaced like some sea creature up for air. And no wonder, considering the events of the last hour.

Zena went to the pantry where the cookies were kept

out of reach, because her mama did not believe in spoiling children by making life too easy for them. In order to get at the cookies, one had to do some climbing, which Zena did with the ease of a cat. On the other hand, milk, which was good for children, was always left in front of your nose, next to the block of ice in the wooden icebox.

"It's hard to talk about," Zena said, clutching a fistful of cookies. "I think I may be shy."

"You? Shy? That will be the day."

This *is* the day, Zena thought, the day my whole life has changed.

"It's about—it's about love I want to talk." It was strange how merely saying the word out loud brought back the lonely and lamenting feeling. Indeed, she seemed all at once to be on an unsettling seesaw of sad and glad.

"*Love?*" Crystal cried and slapped the dough violently. "Oh! Now see what you've gone and made me do! My poor puff paste. Don't you know that puff paste is a very delicate affair? Why in heaven's name couldn't you have waited for a plain yeast dough?"

"I am sorry. Truly. But time and tide wait for no man, and neither does love it seems."

"Stop your foolishness and get to the point," Crystal said crossly.

"First, a nice cup of tea, Crystal?" Zena asked with a buttery voice.

"I suppose so. And while you're at it, make it English tea. Today for a change it has been the Irish in me I've been enjoying, but now I fear it is the English in me I

19

will be needing." Crystal was half Irish and half English and found it a great convenience to use either half as she saw fit.

"Something's gone queer with this puff paste," she murmured. "I don't like the look of it, and it wasn't just my whack that did it. My heart tells me something's gone queer, very queer, with more than my puff paste, very queer . . ."

A lovely shiver went up Zena's spine. Oh, Crystal, if you only knew how right you are.

When the tea was brewed and the puff paste was in the icebox for its final chilling, they sat down at a small table in front of a window. All the windows in this house were heavily curtained except the ones in Crystal's rooms. Crystal said to cook properly she needed to read the sky like a navigator. Red sky at morning might be a warning to a sailor, but to Crystal it could mean no soufflé that day.

Now she yanked the thin muslin curtain to one side. The kitchen was in the back of the house, away from the park, and from there one had a splendid view of dusk descending on brownstone houses, backyards, and beyond them the elevated train which clattered, roared, and thundered up and down Columbus Avenue.

After they had each had a sip of tea, Zena began: "Crystal—"

But Crystal was scanning the sky. "A nice cold wind from the north should have been just the thing for puff paste," she murmured. "Then why wasn't it? *Why* wasn't it?"

"Crystal—about love . . ."

20

Slowly, Crystal came down from the sky to Zena. "Before one word is exchanged, I wish it clearly understood that I was not hired to be an expert on the subject of love." Crystal spoke with uncharacteristic primness.

"But, Crystal, you are one. Aren't you?"

"That is a personal question. No personal questions if you please."

"Do you happen to know anyone who *is* an expert?" Zena almost added "in *this* world," which would have been a dangerous slip of the tongue.

"It's not my place to. I was hired as a cook and a cook I remain, a first class cook my references say. True enough, I have taken the liberty of offering you excellent advice when the occasion warranted, which is the privilege of a family retainer. Perhaps the information you now seek is to be found in *The Book of Knowledge* or, better still, *The Encyclopaedia Britannica*. Who knows? If you look under *L* perhaps you will find *Love*, ducky."

But Zena had been occupied with her own thoughts. "Crystal, do you realize that I have never in my whole life ever seen a real live man and a real live lady really and truly in love with each other? How do you account for that?"

Crystal scratched the corner of her eye. "It could be simply a question of geography. For instance, it is not in the frozen arctic that one sees the bird of paradise, is it?" She shrugged. "Ducky, I don't truthfully have the answer. And me, with all my looking I have never once seen a comet shooting through the skies. It's possible we have both been deprived. I'm not saying we haven't been. You can't have everything."

21

"Well, at least I do so wish I had a papa—"

"Ducky!"

"Well, I do! Why did my papa have to go and die before I was even born?"

"He didn't do it on purpose. It wasn't his fault that the horse bolted and ran away with the carriage. It was just a terrible irony that it was a horse that did it, killed him. But ducky you know the rules as well as I do. We do not talk about your dear dead papa in this house."

"Secrets, secrets, secrets. Nothing but secrets. We don't talk about papa, and we don't talk about money, and now I suppose we won't talk about love—will we?" Quite unlike herself, Zena's voice was on its way to a wail.

Crystal leaned toward her with narrowed eyes. "Ducky, what's come over you since breakfast this morning? You aren't getting odd, are you?"

"How should I know?"

"Or God forbid, *sensitive?* The day that happens I swear I'll give notice. If there's one thing that aggravates me, it's a sensitive girl."

"And what would you do if I turned into a flapper?" Zena asked, only half teasing.

"A flapper? What would I do? Why I'd laugh myself sick, that's what. What a sight you would be with that yellow hair bobbed off and yourself smeared with lipstick and your stockings rolled like a sloven's. The very thought of it makes me sick. No, no, ducky, it's not your style, it isn't for you and that's that. I can tell you one thing, there are no flappers in Buckingham Palace."

"But I'm only a commoner."

22

"Are you now? Let me tell you another thing, we have not come to the end of this story."

"Where I will meet my Own True Love and live happily ever after?"

Crystal fidgeted uneasily in her chair. "I knew it was English tea I would be needing. Say what you will, it is the English in English people that built an empire." She raised her tea cup. "Rule Britannia!"

"In this house you never can get a simple answer to a simple question."

Crystal wasn't listening.

"Zena—you didn't break the rule about strangers today, did you?"

Zena nearly dropped her mama's Royal Worcester tea cup.

"Why, whatever makes you say such a thing?" Zena asked, praying she had succeeded in acting innocent.

"I—I don't know. Things are suddenly very queer, and I don't like it. Something's come over you, hasn't it?"

"Well, maybe it's just the beginning of growing up, and it's making me feel—feel—uh, feel—"

"Anything you feel three times is too much. Too much feeling makes for crow's feet and veins. Princesses, ducky, are taught to feel lightly, with a mere flick of their crested handkerchiefs. Take my advice. Feel lightly, Zena, lightly."

Having given this advice, Crystal looked as if she could use some of it herself: in a house where weeping was forbidden, Crystal's eyes were peculiarly misted.

Zena pretended not to notice. "Since we're speaking

of royalty, I suppose I'd better go to my room and study the succession of English kings." She got up from the chair. "Two Williams, a Henry, a Stephen . . ."

Zena was at the door when Crystal called out.

"Wait!" She walked quickly to Zena. "You're not fooling me," she whispered hoarsely. "I know something's up. I've got my sources. I just want to tell you *one thing*. One thing only. And you had better listen to the warning. Listen! You have an enemy out there—" she pointed out the window, "an enemy who will pretend to be your friend."

Zena stood there with her heart thumping, hammering against her ribs.

"Who is it?" she whispered.

"Never you mind. When the time comes, you will know."

When the time comes . . . time of wonder? Or time of disaster?

Zena started to go.

"Another thing," Crystal said. "You are to tell no one I warned you. It is a terrible big secret, Zena. You are to forget that I ever mentioned it. Is that clear?"

"As mud," Zena cried and ran to her room.

ZENA DID NOT STOP running until she reached the window seat in her room.

This was her own private place. When the silk and satin curtains were drawn back, it was a place with a view of the park, the Plaza, and the castle. Now, it was not an eagle's view she had, but a girl's—half in and half out, half here and half there.

Spread out before her was the park, now a strange night country, its dense blackness punctured only by the pale lights of a few old lampposts. South-southeast was the Plaza with the blaze that enchanted. And remote and brooding over all, the blacker than black shadow of the castle.

Crystal's words of warning whispered through the hush of the house and sent a shiver through her. But I am brave, Zena reminded herself, as she snuggled into

the cushions on the window seat, brave, brave, brave.
. . . With her eyes pulled to the castle, she kept on
exercising bravery.

Then, without being at all drowsy, almost as if she
had been drugged, Zena's head dropped back on a
pillow and she fell into a deep sleep.

It was most unusual. She was not given to naps at
any time and least of all before dinner. It was only a two
minute nap, but it worked wonders. When she woke up,
it was the blaze of the Plaza that was the first thing she
saw. At the sight of it, without any hesitation, she dismissed Crystal's warning as having nothing at all to do
with Jabez. It was just one of the spookier emanations
from Crystal's mysterious past.

That done, Zena returned to the practical business of
love. Where to begin? And what was her hurry? Yes,
there would be Jabez when the time came. But that was
then and this was now and she had a most impatient,
impulsive, and impetuous nature, apparently one as
eager to love, as to be loved.

So . . . where to begin?

Zena turned away from the window and studied her
room. Here?

It was a room, everyone agreed, that was fit for a
princess. It was a room, she thought, that bloomed too
girlishly, too pinkishly. Whatever could be pink was
pink—the silk and satin curtains, the ruffled lamp
shades, the roses strewn across the white painted furniture. The trouble was that pink was not her color. You
either were a pink person or you weren't. To be sure,

pink people had many virtues that she lacked. (They could sew a fine seam, and she could not.) And it went without saying, that pink was for girls. But what she herself knew—blindfolded—was that it took more than pink to make a girl out of a girl. She knew that she, Zena, did not need pink; this much she knew.

It was sea green that was her own true color, the color of adventure on high seas in clear, sparkling sunlight. It also happened to be the true color of her eyes, which, however, turned blue when she was sad and black when she was angry. She had already discovered that it took a bit of doing to hang on to one's own true color.

Especially with a Tribunal of Mamas to contend with. It was a tribunal made up of Mama, whose name was Augusta, and Mama's sisters, Benedicta and Cassandra. Biologically speaking, Benedicta and Cassandra were not mamas at all; they were Old Maids.

Be that as it may, it was Benedicta who was the Mama in charge of Womanliness, under which came Goodness, Sweetness and Light, and Cleanliness. (It was Benedicta who had caught Mama in one of her rare weak moments and was responsible for all the pinkness.) Benedicta worried about Peace—in the family, that is—and Kind Thoughts and Floors Clean Enough to Eat Off. In spite of so much Goodness, Aunt Benedicta meant well.

Cassandra was the Mama in charge of Etiquette and Education: She knew all there was to know about protocol, the seating arrangements for weddings and funerals, particularly the latter, and which schools did the best finishing job. It was she who had picked Miss De Koven's School for Young Ladies where one learned how to accept an invitation from a Duchess to tea (just in case) and how to decline one from a Lady of Questionable Reputation (no matter how interesting that might be). Aunt Cassandra was a person who annoyed people.

And her very own mama? This Mama ruled from a distant throne, a strange place, and, more than likely, a lonely one. This Mama, who was famous for making money, often was away on her travels. But when she was at home, she was also away; at home or abroad, Mama was far away. Wherever she was, she was the Mama in charge of everyone and of all things big and little, of character and bravery and pride and similar prickly subjects.

But surely not of love.

"Love?" That was a word she had never once heard Mama use. That was a word that would very likely embarrass Mama, the way personal questions and compliments did. Behind Mama's brilliant jet eyes were many black pools marked "Private. Keep out."

Clearly, the trail to love would not begin here in this house.

But if not here, then where?

At Du Barry's it turned out.

I N A ROUNDABOUT WAY it was etiquette that led to Du Barry's that day, which only proves that there is more to a proper education than reading, writing, and arithmetic. Quite naturally, at Miss De Koven's School for Young Ladies etiquette was on the required curriculum, and it included learning to curtsy gracefully and demurely to one's elders. It was the curtsy that did it.

"Young ladies," Miss Tittleworth, the Latin teacher, had announced, "the class is dismissed. *Ave atque vale!*"

But the young ladies, as they were always called at Miss De Koven's to keep the goal in mind, were not dismissed until they had formed a pretty line according to height, and one by one had touched the tips of Miss Tittleworth's fingers and curtsied. Since Miss Tittleworth held her fingers up in a delicate curve close to her chin, and since the first in line was the shortest and the fattest girl in the class, who could not always manage the leap up and the dip down without landing on the floor, the pretty line often ended up in hysterical disarray.

So it did that day.

Outside Miss Tittleworth's room, Zena's best friend Vera, who had laughed so much she gasped for breath, cried:

"Oh! Oh! My stomach, it hurts so I can't stand it."

"What you need is a good chocolate parfait at Du Barry's," Zena said firmly and took her friend Vera in hand.

Walking briskly toward Du Barry's, Zena's thoughts were on the chocolate parfait about to be swirled out of parfait glass with parfait spoon, when she heard Vera say: "Bernice cried last night."

Bernice was Vera's older sister. She was nineteen years old and watched birds on the Palisades with some other ex-Girl Scouts. Vera was pretty, and their brother Dickey not only went to Yale, but was handsome. Poor Bernice was homely, but usually cheerful.

"What was she crying about?" Zena asked.

"Marriage."

"*Marriage?*" Goodness, Zena thought, it's an epidemic.

"Mama said Bernice is a hopeless case. Mama said Bernice will never find a husband if she keeps on refusing to go to dances. Mama said watching birds might be all right *after* you have a husband, but it was positively no way to *find* one. Bernice said she was sick of being *the* wallflower of the season. Her friends could jolly well have their coming out parties without her as their mascot. And besides, who needed a husband anyway when there were still so many warblers left to identify when just once to see a myrtle warbler was her heart's desire? That's when Mama had hysterics. Later, when I peeked into Bernice's room it was awful. She sat there with her Audubon book on her lap and big fat tears plopped onto a warbler."

"Oh poor, poor Bernice. Does she really want a husband that badly?"

"Of course. Doesn't everyone?"

Zena stopped walking. She was very fond of poor Bernice. Most probably, she, Zena, was the only person in the whole world who could help poor Bernice. Presto! like that! But Jabez had said he was to be kept a secret or he would disappear. Moreover, even if that were not so, was she generous enough to share Jabez with anyone else? She decided she was not, not even with poor Bernice.

"Come *on*, Zena. What are you dawdling for? There won't be any tables left at Du Barry's if we don't hurry."

They hurried. But Zena felt guilty. On the other hand, she told herself, we're none of us perfect, thank heaven. Perfection was Zena's one and only allergy. It made her itch.

Du Barry's being one of *the* places to go for tea, it was crowded. However, two ladies trailing aigrettes from their velvet hats and exuding Djer Kiss powder vacated a tiny round table for two. Zena and Vera boldly outran two seniors from Miss De Koven's in what Zena was to regard as one of the more significant sprints of her life.

It was while sitting at that particular table having a chocolate parfait and three pieces of French pastry that Zena heard ". . . love . . ." One table away, in spite of being an expert eavesdropper, she could not have caught it. Too much hubbub. Quite possibly it was another miracle, because the two British gentlemen dripping mustaches, exuding Yardley's, and discussing the shooting of grouse in Scotland with their English accents drooping with boredom, did not appear to be likely candidates for eavesdropping on. It was their sudden silence that first attracted her.

"Jolly good" she heard one of them finally mumble.

An inquisitive glance told her it was a Napoleon that so pleased this gentleman.

"He may have lost the battle, but I say, he does rather live on in this little sweet, don't you agree, old chap?" he continued.

"Quite. One must admit that they're masters at it."

"Quite. Masters at what, old chap? Surely not battles?"

"Hardly. Pastry, old chap. Pastry and *l'amour*, I'm told."

"*L'amour*? I say, isn't that French for love?"

"Quite. The French are acknowledged masters at it. So I've been told."

"Acknowledged masters at love? It's jolly well no

wonder they lose battles."

"Quite."

They fell silent again.

Zena's green eyes had fired to emerald with excitement.

L'amour! L'amour! Leave it to these acknowledged masters to have such a beautiful word for love.

She stuffed the last crumb of her chocolate eclair into her mouth and told the bewildered Vera that she must run right home.

Racing to keep up with her, Vera called out: "Zena, I think I smell a secret that you're keeping from me."

Not inclined to answer, Zena kept right on running.

Fortunately, she had just begun to study the language of these fortunate people. Between Chardenal's *Complète* French Course and Madame Duvant—who was guiding them through the good pencils and the bad pens, the good water and the bad ink of Monsieur Chardenal's grammatical world—she would surely get her first marvelous lesson in love.

She found the magic word in Lesson 28: *Aimer* the beautiful verb to love. Oh, verbs, verbs, how she could learn to love them. Her heart leaped expectantly.

It sank when she saw that M. Chardenal could think of no better object to love than white flowers: *Aimez-vous les fleurs blanches?* Who cared about white flowers at a time like this? Anyway, the answer to that question was that she hated lilies, but loved orange blossoms. Could it be that Lesson 28 was not advanced

33

enough for her purpose? Normally no scholar, she studiously flipped pages until she came to the end of the book. M. Chardenal was a big flop. As far as she could make out, M. Chardenal, like her *bonne maman* and the other *mamans*, did not consider love a fit topic for *les enfants*. For all she knew, M. Chardenal was only half French.

When one seeks a fact about such a matter as love, persistence is everything.

There was still Madame Duvant herself—more or less in the flesh. Madame was the only live French person Zena knew, and she would have to do, in spite of the funereal combination of black pompadour stuffed all around her head, black moustache, and long black cotton dress. She never smiled; she never called anyone by name—just *Mademoiselle-là, Mademoiselle-ci.* She moved on legless feet in a dark orbit of her own. It was quite possible that she did not have a heart. But she was French and, astonishingly enough, she was a Madame and not a Mademoiselle, and where there was a breath of life there was hope.

The next morning when the bell rang for French, Zena moved herself from her inconspicuous seat in the last row—where one could daydream and doodle in peace—to one in the first row, directly in the line of fire. A shiver of excitement ran through the class: What was that Zena up to this time?

Unsmiling, legless, Madame Duvant rolled in and went to her desk. Without so much as a "Good morning," she announced the morning's lesson: "*Être.* The verb *to be*." From Madame's lips, it could just as well have been the verb "to die."

Undaunted, Zena glued her eyes to her subject. She started at the bottom, the tip of the worn black boot, gave Madame the benefit of a well turned ankle, and almost couldn't get past the bulge of Madame's stomach. Love, Zena reasoned, ought surely to keep one lean in the stomach. Her incurable optimism, however, sent her onward and upward. Alas, there, where there *should* be a bulge, it was flat as the western plains. (Flat chests had not yet become all the rage.) There was left the face: Not the schoolteacher's plain and dour face, but the one beneath it, the one that had sometime, in a sunnier time, someplace, received the broad gold wedding band on her left hand. In order to uncover the face she sought while Madame swiveled from pupils to desk to blackboard, Zena had to wriggle, ceaselessly. Her classmates were in an agony of suppressed giggles, and notes were flying under desks toward Zena.

She ignored them. She unwound the black hair of Madame, rearranged it into a soft coif, dressed her in white muslin, gave her a straw bonnet with satin ribbons long enough to swing coquettishly over her arm, and tried, with all the power she had, to give her the face of a young girl. She went so far as to walk her through the Bois in the springtime with a shadowy— but handsome, handsome—young grenadier. . . .

Madame, unfortunately, was not there in the Bois, but here in the classroom. Little by little, Madame had become aware of Zena's examination: Her hand flew to her hair; she felt for the buttons at her waist; the color came up into her face in thick red patches. She pounced on Zena.

"*Mademoiselle-ci!* Give me the negative interrogative of *être. Vite!*"

Zena floated up from her seat. She recited "*Ne suis-je pas?*" with such emotion, so tremulously imploring an answer to the essential question—am I not? are you not? are we not? are they not?—that, at her conclusion, Madame mopped her moustache beaded with perspiration. And Zena's classmates, bewildered but still loyal, twittered with approval. But for once it had not been Zena's intention to amuse: She simply had been the prisoner of her *idée fixe.*

Madame rapped her desk with her ruler. "*Mademoiselle-ci*, you will leave this room."

"Who me?" Zena asked, genuinely puzzled.

"But I do not mean your brother or your sister. You. You. Out. *Vite!*"

"But Madame . . ."

Madame broke her ruler.

Zena left.

Outside, in the gloomy hall of the old brownstone where the murmuring of young ladies learning sounded mournful and futile, Zena tasted the cold, heavy pudding of injustice.

When the bell rang, her classmates filed past her, not quite as loyal as they had been: What the *heck* had she been up to?

At last, after a long wait, Madame herself came out

and beckoned Zena back into the deserted classroom.

Madame was weeping. Zena stood before her, her head bowed with regret. It was also bowed to spare Madame the embarrassment of weeping publicly.

"Mademoiselle, you are a cruel girl. You have made the joke out of a poor old woman. You have no heart!"

"No heart? Oh, Madame, you are wrong about that—"

"Impertinent too! Quiet! You must learn a lesson. *Vite!* You must learn a lesson in love."

Ah! At last!

"Oh, Madame! *Mais oui, oui, oui,*" Zena sang out, so excited she spoke French without knowing it, "*merci, Madame, merci beaucoup—*"

Madame wheezed from pain or fright. She opened her desk drawer and shuffled an untidy mess of needles and threads, rumpled used handkerchiefs, an opened box of biscuits, papers and pencils, until she found a bottle of smelling salts. She inhaled deeply, holding on to the top of her head.

Only barely revived, Madame went to the blackboard and, with a hand shaking so violently she broke three pieces of chalk before she could steady it, she wrote the magic word *Aime* in her slanted French script; then she turned to see whether she had the attention of this intractable pupil.

Indeed she did.

So much so that it caused her to break another piece of chalk before she continued with *ton prochain comme toi même.* For once forgetting to be frugal, she flung the chalk from her, wheeled, and shouted:

"Mademoiselle, translate! *Vite!*"

"Love," Zena sang softly and slowly, reluctant to part with the lovely liquid flow of this word. She stopped: Now *who* could *prochain* be?

"Oh, Madame, I do not know *prochain*," she said. "Who, Madame, is *prochain?*" she asked, longing to make his acquaintance.

"But of course you would not know. This is the point of this lesson. And you will learn it. You will write this commandment down one hundred and one times. This commandment, Mademoiselle, you must obey it, always, you must make it your life's work. This commandment, Mademoiselle, is translated into your heartless language thus—'Thou shalt love thy *neighbor* as thyself.' *Maintenant*, write! *En français!* 'Aime ton prochain comme toi même.' Vite!*"

Zena wrote, holding back tears of disappointment. Neighbors, Madame, are not what I had in mind, she said to herself. As far as the eye can see, Madame, there is not one neighbor who could become one's Own True Love.

And so she said goodbye to the French, leaving them across the sea with all their secrets intact. It was a sad parting, but there was the comfort of knowing that when all else failed—by which she meant these solo flights—waiting to help there would be Jabez.

Before she went to sleep that night, she opened the window of her bedroom and leaned out. A late harvest moon hung low over the park, and the lights of the city were little golden apples espaliered against the black silhouettes of the buildings.

She heard the night doorman whistle for a taxi. She heard the coquettish laughter of flappers. She heard the laughter of lionized young men.

The better to see, the better to hear, she leaned dangerously far out the window. Where were they off to, these most beautiful people? What magical place? Oh, wait for baby, wait for Zena, wait for me.

Perhaps it was her bat's eye vision that made the lionized young men and the flappers seem extraordinarily unsteady on their feet, swaying and bumping into each other. She decided it was. She decided they were swaying and bumping as if they were riding a fast train headed for a beautiful life, a free one. One day she would be on it too.

Across the avenue, the shadowy figure of a tall boy glided slowly past the dark trees. Dark as it was, it was unmistakably a boy hunched in deep thought. "Whoopee!" one of the flappers shrilled. The boy stopped with one foot off the ground. He too looked and listened. A moonbeam picked him up and Zena could see spikes of hair sticking up like the ragged crest of a kingfisher. And then he caught sight of her hanging out the window. He raised a hand; it could have been in greeting or warning. It was too dark to tell. Not knowing why, Zena pulled herself in and sank into the cushions of the window seat.

She heard the taxi pull up. She heard the tumbling laughter as they got in. She had wanted to see them go off into their beautiful night. If it hadn't been for that boy she would have.

Oh, Jabez, envoy extraordinary and minister plenipotentiary of love, remember me when the time comes, teach me the words and the songs and the ways. Your humble servant, Zena.

She bowed to the east where the castle stood, seeming in the full light of the moon to belong to the moon's country.

CHAPTER 5

LOVE AS A VOCATION had come to Zena out of
season, in the early fall. The overdose of generosity came with the first snow.

Love, if it were allowed to do so, she already suspected, could be very time consuming; it might also get
in the way of fun. It could; but she would make sure it
did not.

So, the day the first snow fell, Zena had her mind on
snow, only snow.

That Friday, it had been presumed that Zena would
spend the early part of the afternoon in the basement of
a neighborhood church watching Miss De Koven's basketball team play one from Miss Bentworth's School for
Young Ladies, after which she would keep a quite unnecessary appointment to have her excellent teeth
checked. But in that basement, where the odors of coal,

sneakers, serge bloomers, and the gym teacher's Life Buoy soap rose from the dampness, word came that it was snowing—and sticking.

When De Koven made its first basket and the cheers of D-E-K-O-V-E-N is The School for Me shrilled through the chilly basement, Zena crawled behind the leaping bloomers to make her exit.

The snow was falling. Zena lifted her face to it, put her tongue out to catch a snow flake, and went to the nearest phone to cancel the dentist appointment.

Free, she went to the park to see what she could see, and to hitch a ride on someone's sled. In the fall of snow, the park was all picture post cards and a wonderful crazy quilt of trees and light and shadows; now the castle rising above it was a medieval painting. Everything was a delightful something else.

She rounded a bend in the path and came upon the sledding slope. She stood still. Always a one for collecting lovely moments for future reference, she wanted to take it in—the bobbing, sliding, careening sleds and the shouts and the shrieks and the laughter.

A girl with a red tam o'shanter came tearing down the hill as if she were fleeing a dragon, and she heard her name wailing over the laughter.

"Zee-na, Zee-na . . ."

It was Vera, who had not gone to the basketball game at all that day.

"What's happened?" Zena asked.

"Something terrible."

"For goodness sake, is it a matter of life or death?"

"It's worse than that. Oh, Zena, I'm with a boy."

A boy? A b-o-y boy? This was indeed a big piece of news. What with Miss De Koven's School for Young Ladies and the Mamas' distaste for strangers, boys were paper figures in the scenes of one's childhood—animated ones to be sure—always racing, fighting, being boyish and fresh, but nothing real about them. True, her Own True Love would be a man, not a boy, but one had to begin at the beginning. A boy ought to do nicely.

"A boy? Why, Vera, that's terrific. Who is he? Is it a date? Are you having a *date?*"

"It isn't terrific at all, it's terrible. I don't know one word to say to him and I'm getting sick. Hot and cold and shivery all over. He's somebody's brother, a friend of Dickey's—and I need help."

"Haven't you said one word to him?"

"I asked him what school he went to. He told me. He asked me what school I went to. I told him. I asked him what his favorite subject was. He said math. I said I hated math. Maybe I shouldn't have, but I did. I said wasn't the snow pretty. He said it was okay. Oh, God, what else is there to say?"

Plenty. Zena saw the word streak across her brain, as unexpected and miraculous as Jabez.

"Can I be of any help to you?" Zena asked, keeping her fingers crossed for the right answer.

She got it. "Yes," Vera said. "Come back with me. *Please*. Just for a minute. *Please.*"

She had her faults, but she was loyal and kind-hearted, wasn't she? Especially to a best friend? Oh, she was. So Zena went with her friend without further ado. But trudging up the hill, she did wonder why Vera, who was such a pretty girl and who had a brother Dickey who went to Yale, was in such trouble. Surely, she should have absorbed some conversation from a Yale man who was in her own family? As for herself, perhaps she was being vainglorious (a word she had not expected to use so soon), but she did not expect conversation to be her problem. On the other hand, accidents will happen and what if she too should be stricken dumb? Considering everything, the sooner she found this out the better. She tugged at Vera to climb more quickly.

A young boy sat on a sled with his chin gloomily cupped in his hand. Slowly, but politely, he stood up (he was a short boy) and kept his eyes down.

"This is my friend, Zena—the girl I was calling to," Vera squeaked. "This is—this is Philip."

Zena took her kid-gloved hand out of her coat pocket.

"Hello, Philip," she said, and was relieved at the ease with which the words flowed.

Philip went white, and she put her hand back in the pocket.

He made a noise that was a cross between the hungry bark of a seal and the angry chatter of a squirrel. He cleared his throat. He looked up quickly, ready to look down again. But he didn't look down again: His eyes remained up. They were dazed. He managed to extend a woolen gloved hand.

Zena took her hand out again. They shook hands.

And she smiled. All over. Conversation was not going to be the problem.

Not for her.

"And whose beautiful Flexible Flyer is this? Yours, Philip?" A trifle too coy perhaps, but then she was only a beginner.

"Mine," Philip said.

"Ah, I thought so. There's something different about it. Different from the ordinary Flexible Flyer, I mean." Well, there was; in this light; in this place.

Philip took a long time looking at his sled. He shrugged. "New."

Zena leaned over and slid the handle bars back and forth.

"It certainly is flexible. I'll bet this sled is fast as the wind and you'd better know what you're doing when you steer it."

"Ride?"

Zena remembered Vera—reluctantly. She glanced toward her inquiringly. Vera said: "Go!" Perhaps it was only Zena's imagination, but it sounded somewhat sharp.

"Philip, I would love to ride with you on your sled."

"Okay."

Philip stretched out on the sled, holding it still with his toes dug into the snow. Zena waved gaily to Vera and settled herself on top of him.

"Take the steep way, Philip," she said.

He shoved hard with his feet, and they were off. He took her at her word, and they went bellywhopping

45

down the hill, skinning past other sleds, a tree or two, not missing a single rise or bump.

At the end of the ride, she pushed her hat back in place and spoke the truth as it appeared to her then and there. "That ride was the most thrilling thing that ever happened to me in my life. You are a wonderful sledder, Philip, and I certainly thank you."

He almost smiled. "Wrists," he said, pulling the sled back up the hill.

"Wrists?" She hurried to keep up with him.

"Strong wrists. Easy."

"Oh no, Philip, it takes more than wrists to sled the way you do. Do you know what it takes?"

"Tell me."

"Spunk. S-P-U-N-K. Spunk. You're an unusually spunky person, if you don't mind my saying so."

Then, right there in Central Park, there was a most curious happening.

Philip's shoulders went back; his head went up; he looked Zena straight in the eye and kept on looking at her. And, himself surprised, he touched his shoulder where he would have been tapped. Then his hand went to his hip where the sword would be. There was no question about it: Right there in front of her eyes was a boy who had just been knighted. By her.

If she had just turned the pumpkin into the golden coach and four, Zena could not have been more amazed. Could she possibly have done this all by herself? Or had someone else . . . ? The thought made her look behind her. "Jabez . . . ?" she mouthed. There was no answer. Well then. . . . Watching this boy being knighted, Zena knew how Beethoven felt when da, da, da—*da* turned out to be the Fifth Symphony: awed and humble too.

"Don't mind—Zena." The boy gulped some badly needed air and started to talk. He talked and he talked and he talked. He talked about spunk, his; he talked about math—algebra, geometry, trigonometry, and calculus; he talked as if he had been storing words from the day he was born.

In the future, perhaps she would be obliged to knight with a lighter touch.

Just before they reached the top of the hill where Vera waited for them, stamping her feet to keep warm, her little face pinched, he asked her if they couldn't let Vera have this wonderful sled all to herself, while they went to Du Barry's for a hot chocolate.

It was one of those moments, and she knew it.

Love or loyalty?

Zena chose loyalty. Hands down. Thinking about it later, she wanted to be honest with herself. Perhaps it was because math was decidedly not her subject either. Perhaps it was easy when it was quite unlikely that the person would turn out to be your Own True Love. Whatever it was, she knew that loyalty was lovely, but what would one do when love was lovelier?

As she said her farewells, loyalty bred generosity: "Philip, Vera is famous for being a wonderful listener."

And generosity, it seemed, was like eating peanuts, once started it couldn't be stopped.

She had taken only a few steps when she bumped into Bernice. Literally, because Bernice stepped out from behind a sycamore. As always, binoculars hung from Bernice's neck and rested on her chest as if they had sprung from her body, a premium from nature that had otherwise been stingy.

"Oh. Bernice, what were you looking for behind that tree?"

The cold was horrid to Bernice. It pinched her homeliness into a purple caricature of itself. To make it worse, she was once again sad.

"Um—ah. Nothing in particular. Just looking. Um—ah—"

It was not like Bernice to be hemming and hawing. Bernice was a direct and hearty person. A terrible thought crossed Zena's mind. Bernice wasn't about to pine away for want of a husband, was she?

"What is that flying way up there?" Zena asked, intending to distract Bernice from husbands and back to birds.

Barely lifting her eyes, Bernice said: "That, Zena, is nothing but a pigeon."

"Sorry."

"That's all right. You may not know birds—but you seem to know something else."

"I do?"

"So it seems. I really didn't mean to spy, Zena, but I couldn't help seeing the strangeness with Philip—"

"Oh, you saw that?" (So it really had happened; it had not been just a trick of her imagination.)

"How could I help it? It was in my field." She pointed to the glasses. "Zena—I do so long to know—what did you do? What did you say? What was the—what was the magic secret? Please forgive me for prying—but what *happened?*"

Zena now knew what a quandary was. She was both perplexed and doubtful. She doubted that she ought to come right out and say she had simply knighted Philip. In the first place, it might sound conceited. And secondly, for all she knew, in a democracy there might be some law against knighting people. Constitutional law was not one of her strong points. Then there was the more important question of the secret behind the power to knight people. Was it Jabez? Or was it the magical offshoot of her pursuit of love? Whatever it was, her instinct told her that the answer should be another secret, one best kept even from her own self.

Yet here in front of her nose was poor Bernice so desperately in need of help she was about to cry again.

Zena fingered the deck of Old Maid that went whereever she went these days, usually in a pocket, sometimes in a pocketbook or muff, once strapped to her waist with adhesive as if she were a spy bearing secret documents.

"Zena, you aren't angry at me for asking, are you?"

"Of course not, Bernice." Zena spoke very slowly. Generosity was bubbling up like an uncorked bottle of soda pop; soon it would be fizzing all over the place. She would try to change the subject. "Tell me, Bernice, don't you still want to see a myrtle warbler more than anything else in the whole world?"

Bernice burst into tears. Right there in Central Park with the first snow still falling.

That did it. Zena reached up and put her arm around Bernice.

"Oh, poor Bernice, poor, poor Bernice—"

One word does lead to another, and before she knew it, Zena had said the fateful words, "Bernice I will try to help you."

Bernice's weeping came to an asthmatic stop.

"No one on this earth can help me."

"That may be true," Zena conceded, "but I happen to have a friend who—who the less said the better. Bernice, do you trust me?"

Bernice turned her doleful eyes to the place at the foot of the sledding hill where Philip had been knighted.

"I think I do, Zena."

"Then mum's the word. Swear it."

Bernice raised her right hand. "Mum."

"I will do my best," Zena promised. "I may not succeed. You see, my friend is a rather strange person. But one way or another you will be hearing from me."

Feeling more than a little strange herself, Zena headed for a shop that sold candles.

On the way she knighted two boys on purpose, merely to see if she could. One had just been about to fling a snowball at her, and the other she knighted because he was so very threadbare and shivering and miserable in the cold with only a coat sleeve to wipe his poor running nose. (Knighting was excellent for his nose; it dried up immediately. Knighting did more than that: He would become a famous matinee idol when he grew up; the snowball boy would become a famous tycoon; Philip would become a famous math genius who would help send a man to the moon.)

Whatever the secret, the technique apparently was to smile a certain smile and look a certain look. Since she couldn't see herself, there was no describing it, only feeling it. It felt magical.

Meaning to do no more than practice the smile and the look, Zena accidentally knighted a raccoon-coated college boy shuffling through the snow with a flapper. The flapper thought she had either drunk too much bootleg gin or the boy had. She decided the boy had, and she asked him to please go home and take a cold shower and drink a pot of black coffee to sober him up. This hurt the college boy's feelings, but having just been knighted he was very polite about it. The flapper didn't know what to make of the whole business and wished it hadn't happened.

So did Zena. She saw that she would have to mind her knighting.

But now there was the candle to get, the one that would bring Bernice her Own True Love and Happiness Ever After.

What with knighting people left and right and playing fairy godmother to Bernice, it did seem like rather more power than a person her weight and size ought to have. But then, it wasn't exactly her own doing, was it?

CHAPTER 9

THE MOMENT ZENA walked into her house
with the candle hidden under her coat she smelled
trouble. She smelled the disinfectant, which always
clung hygienically to Aunt Benedicta, and the ladylike
perfume favored by both Aunt Cassandra and the
Queen of England.

"*They're* in the parlor searching for dust like it was
arsenic," the parlormaid grumbled, and muttered something about giving notice.

When Mama was away on her travels attending to
her business, which was the making of large amounts of
money, the other two Mamas came to make daily tours
of inspection. Crystal said these tours were unscheduled
in the hope that they would catch someone doing something; any trifling thing would do, hungry as they were
for other people's mistakes. Crystal and these two

Mamas did not like each other.

But there was another smell that rose most alarmingly to join the others. It came from her own self. From its warm hiding place under her coat, the pungent seaside smell of bayberry was escaping. Recklessly unconcerned with smells, she had picked her candle for its color, the lovely yellow that Jabez seemed to favor.

Now this carelessness had trapped her.

"Cassandra, is that Zena we hear?"

What was she to do? In a second they would come out and find her standing there hugging her coat and reeking of guilt.

The clocks. For once, Zena was pleased to be living in a house where time was kept by split seconds as if people were trains. There were clocks wherever one looked. Hastily, she opened the door of the nearest clock, a towering, hectoring grandfather, famous for keeping perfect time, and popped the candle in it. Out of reach of the swinging pendulum, she fervently hoped, as she went to greet the Mamas.

"I for one have always thought it unseemly for Victoria to be sharing a shelf with that Louis XIV," Zena heard Cassandra say as she entered the room the parlormaid had called the parlor, but which Cassandra called the drawing room.

"But dear, if Louis XIV was naughty isn't it unfortunate that his furniture was so pretty?" Benedicta asked with a logic all her own.

The two ladies were inspecting Mama's curio cabinet, where the crowned heads of Europe smiled or pouted or simply stared from tea cups, beer steins, shaving mugs, and plates commemorating their coronations.

"How was Louis naughty?" Zena asked.

Two pairs of pince-nez were nervously pushed back and focused on Zena.

Cassandra and Benedicta's pince-nez were forever plummeting toward soup, other people's frailties, and the news of births, deaths, and marriages in the *Times*. Mama (who only wore hers for reading Zena's report cards and lawyers' letters) kept her pince-nez right where it belonged on the bridge of her haughty nose. But then, Cassandra and Benedicta never could keep up with their sister Augusta. Whereas Mama's hair was worn in a pompadour as sleek as black satin and was all her own, theirs were wispy, dun-colored ones with the rats poking through. Copycatting Mama, so very much richer, so very much smarter than they were, was a losing battle.

There was only one thing they did not care to copy-cat. They did not care to have a child with *yellow* hair. No one, but no one, in their family had ever had such a peculiarity. And as far as anyone knew, no one in *his* (meaning Papa's) family had either.

Cassandra implied that in giving birth to a child with yellow hair, Mama had made a *faux pas* somewhat worse than using the wrong fork; and Benedicta worried about the Goodness of yellow hair: Perhaps in its very pigment it carried a tendency to naughtiness? Behind a hand shielding her mouth, she whispered of persons in the chorus and other ladies of questionable reputation usually being blondes.

Mama would look down her nose at her sisters and accuse them of suffering from a severe case of Zenaphobia, a word they tried in vain to look up in the dictionary.

But Zena noticed that whenever her yellow hair was mentioned, there was a stirring in one of those black pools in Mama's eyes that just possibly could be—*fear?* Mama *afraid?*

"But how *was* Louis naughty?" Zena repeated.

"Good afternoon, Zena," Cassandra said in her most educational voice, the one that forbade all questions.

"Good afternoon, Aunt Cassandra, and good afternoon, Aunt Benedicta," Zena said in her most polite and her kindest voice, the one most likely to please—and to distract from her being questioned.

"Have we forgotten to curtsy?"

Yes, we had. She curtsied.

"And haven't we forgotten something else?" asked Aunt Benedicta sweetly.

No, we had not forgotten to kiss Aunt Benedicta. Today we did not wish to. But since it had become necessary to do so, she could only hope that Aunt Benedicta, who could smell a germ as well as an unkind thought, had a stuffed nose today.

She did not have one.

After Zena dutifully pecked Aunt Benedicta's immaculately scrubbed cheek, Benedicta asked, "Cassandra dear, do we not smell bay rum?" (Benedicta only felt herself to be on sure ground when it came to Goodness,

Sweetness and Light, and Cleanliness; all else was open to question.)

"Bay rum?" Cassandra was shocked. "Zena, come to me."

Zena hesitated; took one or two uncertain steps.

"Closer!" Cassandra ordered.

How explain that it was bayberry, not bay rum? Before she had a chance to improvise, Cassandra said:

"Bay rum is a most unladylike scent. It is used by gentlemen after they shave. Kindly explain how you come to smell of bay rum, Zena."

Zena shrugged. "It's a mystery." In a way it was, wasn't it? Since it all began with Jabez? Besides, how was she to have known that that same berry that would magically bring Jabez, also brought an after shave lotion?

The three of them stood silently locked in this mystery.

Of all unlikely people, Aunt Benedicta was the first to come up with a solution. "I know," she said, herself amazed at her brightness, "it's the dentist."

"The dentist?" Zena and Cassandra asked together.

Zena had forgotten all about him and the broken appointment. Not knowing what else to do, she decided that honesty was the best policy after all, and she confessed to having gone sleigh riding instead.

"That was very naughty of you, dear," Benedicta said.

"But I've just confessed and told the truth," Zena replied.

"So you did. That was very good of you, dear," Benedicta agreed.

"It isn't polite to break appointments at the last moment," Cassandra said crossly. "Unless you have a suitable excuse. I think she ought to be punished."

"Oh no." Benedicta raised a restraining hand. "I'm sure the child meant no harm."

"I didn't," Zena said, wearying of this whole conversation. "In fact, I meant to do good. I helped a friend in need by going sleigh riding with a boy!" she blurted out.

"A boy!" they chorused.

"A b-o-y boy."

Momentarily confounded, the ladies were silent again.

Again, Benedicta was the first to speak. "Do little boys use bay rum, Cassandra dear?"

For once Cassandra was at a loss; not having made a study of little boys, she had no answer.

Zena had one: "It just so happens that Philip is a mathematical genius. And everyone knows that geniuses make up their own rules and regulations. If a little genius feels like using bay rum, he does. And now, if you will excuse me, I have to do my homework which is, you will be happy to know, Aunt Cassandra, the succession of English kings. Goodbye, Aunt Benedicta and goodbye, Aunt Cassandra." She curtsied and left the room, chanting. "Two Williams, a Henry, a Stephen, a Henry . . ."

A foot or so outside the parlor, Zena stopped chanting

and listened: ". . . isn't her hair yellower than it used to be, dear? . . . do we know any Philip? . . . aren't geniuses even stranger than strangers? . . . Augusta must stop making money long enough to tell her yellow-haired daughter that she is not to go sleigh riding with strangers because in our family *we do not marry strangers . . .*"

Oh, don't we? Zena thought. We'll see about that.

Then she sensed trouble before she knew why. Her eyes flew to the face of the old grandfather clock, then to the next nearest clock. Horrified, she saw that the grandfather clock was ten minutes slower than it ought to be. She opened the door. The pendulum had stopped. But the candle was where she had left it! It had *not* been dislodged by the swinging pendulum and could *not* have stopped the pendulum.

She grabbed the candle, nudged the pendulum into motion, and fled to her room as quickly—and as quietly—as possible.

There, she lifted the cushion of a window seat and hid the candle in the box below, where it joined old roller skates, jump ropes, and tops.

That done, Zena collapsed on the floor and thought that life was getting rather complicated for a person her age.

What had stopped the clock? Or was it *who?* If it was Jabez, it was a devil of a way to keep himself secret. And, if it was Jabez, what in the world was he up to?

She stretched out on the Aubusson rug and, surrounded by pale green leaves and shell pink roses, she thrust aside all cause for alarm. That night there would be the candle to light, a beautiful complication. (She did have to admit that she enjoyed complications, the simple life apparently not being to her taste.)

Which reminded her that she did indeed have to memorize the succession of English kings.

She was at her desk twiddling her yellow hair and murmuring, "Two Williams, a Henry, a Stephen, a Henry, a Richard, a John, a Henry . . ." when throughout the house the clocks struck five o'clock.

She had been waiting for this. She tiptoed to the kitchen. At five o'clock, Crystal would be in her room changing from her afternoon uniform to her evening one, as would the chambermaid, the parlormaid, and the waitress.

The kitchen was the only room in this house where one could find a match, and Zena needed a match. Just to play safe, she grabbed three.

She would also need a candle holder. Why hadn't she thought of that before? She raced around the vast kitchen opening and closing cupboards. She settled on an egg cup sprinkled with rosebuds, part of a breakfast set no longer in use. Fortunately, the rosebuds were pink; yellow would have been too perfect.

Safely back in her room, she hid the matches and the egg cup in the box with the candle. She was shuffling through the deck of Old Maid and had forgotten all about the singular behavior of the grandfather clock when she was recalled to it with a shock.

Ten minutes past the hour, into the deep hush of the

house there crashed the sound of a clock striking the hour in aberrant solitude.

Zena heard the rush of feet toward the entrance hall. She must not rush; she must compose herself for an inquisition. This was accomplished by counting to one hundred by tens, a procedure much practised.

Cassandra and Benedicta were in the entrance hall with their coats on, ready to leave. Crystal was there; so were the parlormaid, the chambermaid, the waitress, the laundress, the scrub woman, the floor waxing man, and the window cleaner.

They were all staring at the grandfather clock.

The door bell rang. Everyone jumped.

"Open the door," Crystal ordered the parlormaid.

Reluctantly, the parlormaid obeyed.

Franklin, Mama's fat chauffeur, stood there with Mama's best fur coat over one arm, Mama's dressing case in one hand, and Mama's suitcase in the other hand.

Behind him stood Mama.

"Move, why don't you?" Mama said to Franklin's back.

"I—I will do my best, Madam."

It was a large entrance hall, but it was crowded. Franklin was very fat, but he managed to squeeze into a place as close to the exit as possible. Franklin was timid and his eyes rolled apprehensively around the assembled group.

Mama entered. When Mama entered *any* room, she made an entrance. Mama wearing her least good fur coat, the one she used only for riding in her automobiles, was still an impressive figure. Her black eyes swept across them like a scythe, leaving the strong impression that heads had already been sent rolling.

"How kind of you," Mama said in her softest and coolest and most Mama-ish voice, "to have left your duties to greet me. How very kind. But will someone tell me quickly what this is all about. Quickly!"

They all pointed toward the clock. Mama looked, and her eyes narrowed.

"Augusta, your favorite, most reliable clock is ten minutes slow," Cassandra informed her sister, not without a faint note of triumph. "Your clocks are never slow." With unblinking eyes, she brought the slowness of this clock down on Zena's yellow head.

"I can read quite as well as you can, Cassandra. I see you and Benedicta were about to leave. Pray do not let me keep you. Franklin, you will kindly drive my sisters home. The rest of you now have my permission to return to your duties."

It was her daughter who now got her full attention, rather more clinical than maternal. Without taking her eyes from Zena, she said: "Crystal—how are you?"

"I am well, madam," Crystal said slowly, *her* eyes on the clock. "As well as can be expected—madam."

Mama's eyes narrowed again. "Oh," she said. "Have we had any visitors?"

"Not exactly, madam."

Life, Zena decided, was not only complicated and getting more so, but was also getting more and more mysterious.

Mama nodded, and Crystal left them alone.

"Hello, Mama," Zena said, smiling. She was always happy to see Mama home from her travels, but it would have been better if Mama had waited one more day to come home, after she had stopped smelling from bayberry and certainly after the candle had been lit. It was going to be risky doing that now.

"Let me look at you," Mama was saying.

Zena stood straight and tall. Mama took a good look, but gave no sign of pleasure or displeasure at what she saw. Before too long, Zena hoped to find out whether or not she was pretty. So far this too had been kept a secret.

"Have your aunts been pleased with your behavior?"

"No, Mama."

"No, Mama?"

"No. I smell of bayberry, and I went sleigh riding with a boy named Philip who is a mathematical genius and whose brother is a friend of Dickey who goes to Yale University, which is in New Haven, Connecticut."

Mama pulled off her gloves, kid finger by kid finger, and took off her worst fur coat. She unhooked the pince-nez clipped to her dress and fastened them on to her nose. She studied her daughter intently for what seemed to her daughter to be forever. Then her eyes traveled to the clock that was ten minutes slow.

With her eyes still on the clock, Mama said, "In our family we do not smell of bayberry, and we do not go sleigh riding with *strange boys* whatever their credentials including the geography of their brothers' universities. You will do well to remember that in the future.

Zena, do you know what a duenna is?"

"No, Mama."

"It is a chaperon who goes with a young lady wherever she goes and sees to it that the young lady behaves like one. Always. How would you feel about having one?"

"I would hate it, Mama."

"So would I. I was my own duenna." Mama regarded her daughter, sadly this time. "Now I will kiss you."

Mama only kissed Zena hello and goodbye, rarely inbetween, and always in private. That was the way Mama was. Zena was certain she was the least kissed person in the whole world, except for orphans . . . of which she was one-half.

Mama kissed Zena in her usual way, lightly on the forehead. "Indeed you do smell of bayberry." Then Mama did, what was for Mama, the unusual: She took Zena into her arms and hugged her tightly, protectively. When she released Zena she said: "It smells of trouble, bayberry does."

There were people who thought Mama was psychic.

The door was locked and only a tiny night light glowed in a far corner, casting strange shadows on the tile floor. As she tiptoed across the room, Zena thought that a less appropriate place for the evocation of romance would be hard to find. Some isolated gazebo in a moonlit glade should have been the place; but since none was at hand, one had to be practical even about romance.

Fortunately, the bathroom was very large. To get from the marble basin to the tub, raised high on fluted feet, one could gambol, or waltz, or, as Zena frequently did, one could tango. It was a place where by morning the telltale smell of bayberry would be overpowered by the prevailing ones of castile soap, glycerine and rose water, and Dr. Lyon's tooth powder. But most importantly, it was the one room in the house that it was more seemly to lock than to leave open.

Zena set the candle in the egg cup and sat down on the cold floor with it. Her heart thumped wildly as she lit it.

Now, the shadows, which had been merely strange, became grotesque beings dancing in a frenzy on the ceiling, the walls, and the floor. It was as if one were in a cave—or was it a catacomb?

She took a deep breath, inhaling bayberry as she did so, and held the card over the flame.

"*J*—?" Her voice was strange and far away.

The flame sputtered and flared as if it were about to devour the card. She pulled the card away and saw that one corner was scorched. At the thought that if she were not careful her whole life could literally go up in flames, she sternly commanded herself to *keep calm* and *think*.

What exactly had Jabez meant by "giving each letter its *proper* due?"

Not even the faintest question mark is allowed, Jabez?

The flame hissed.

"Oh, please," she said, "I do believe, I do."

And then with her conviction strong and declarative, she began again: "*J*—"

The letter *J* disappeared.

And one by one, as she gave each letter its proper due, they disappeared until all that was left was "Matchmaker" and "By Appointment to Their Majesties, The Kings and Queens of Many Realms."

The flame flickered and began to get smaller and smaller until it almost disappeared, seeming to pull the card down with it. Then up it shot, blazing with a brilliant red that spread over the room.

Zena kept her eyes fixed on the card.

Gradually, the red of the flame faded to shades of rose, turned bluish pink, and finally mauve.

And in this mauve light, seen almost as if through water, the legend appeared: *The castle tomorrow dusk.*

Zena gazed at the card in her fingers, transfixed. Then, before her eyes, one by one, all the letters disappeared until all that was left in her hand was a blank card.

The candle went out by itself.

The castle tomorrow dusk.

CHAPTER 7

A T DUSK THE CASTLE was deserted. The wintry clouds pressing down on the tower were dark with doom and storms ahead. And all around the castle, as if it were a moat, yesterday's fall of snow—now mauve as the dusk itself—lay undisturbed, unmarked by so much as a bird or a squirrel or a cat.

Zena turned her back on the castle and faced west, the direction Jabez should be coming from. Listening for a footstep, she didn't hear the sounds of the city beyond the park, only the eerie creaking of a tree close by.

Almost before she saw it, she felt the shadow on the snow. The cat's shadow. He came silently, the black cat with the yellow eyes, circled her three times and stretched out in front of her, blocking her way. It was as if he had stalked his prey and were holding it captive.

But the cat had not come from the west. Could it have

come from the castle? She bent over to trace its paw marks.

She froze.

Black against the mauve snow were the toes of a man's shoes, shoes topped by black spats. The shoes did not move, not by so much as a hair's breadth. And neither did Zena.

"They are made for me in London by the best bootmaker in *this* world. Are you quite finished admiring them?"

Zena straightened up slowly. Jabez was much taller than she remembered. His black fedora was dipped low over his eyes, and a coat lined with fur replaced the chesterfield, fur so soft and rich it could only be sable.

"Good—good evening," she managed to say and even remembered to curtsy.

He barely nodded; his face was as wintry as the scene.

"Sir—sir, is something wrong?"

"Of course. There always is. Isn't there?" he snapped.

"Yes sir."

"Who taught you that?"

"Why you did, sir, just this very minute."

"Stop that!"

"Stop what?" Zena asked with increasing alarm and confusion.

"Stop being so damn susceptible. I simply can't have each and every tentative fancy of mine take root and flower into the eighth wonder of the world. Can I?"

"No sir."

"Then stop that knighting business. At once."

"So it *was* you, sir, who gave me the power?"

"Of course. You didn't think you came by it naturally, did you? With *your* genes?"

"No sir, I didn't. I thought it was you, and I do want to thank you from the bottom of my heart. I think it's a perfectly lovely power. Why do you want me to stop knighting people? I should think you would be very proud to have it work so well."

"It isn't working well at all. It's premature. It's indiscriminate. It's overdone. And it isn't meant to be a conjurer's trick. It was a mistake, and I take it all back. That is, I want *you* to take it all back."

"Excuse me, sir, but if you're the one who did it, why can't you undo it?"

In the look Jabez gave Zena there was puzzlement and perhaps even awe.

"An interesting question," he murmured, "very interesting. As I said before, you are too susceptible. Be that as it may, I do not wish to have any more knighting, nor do I wish there to be any more sleigh riding with strange boys—"

Zena broke in: "Funny. That's just what my mama said—"

"Every once in a long time, your mama and I see eye to eye. Be that as it may, if I am to be your matchmaker, I retain the exclusive right to make the match for you. I do not care to have the clutter, the confusion, and the complications of a horde of would-be suitors. I am too busy for complications. For you, strange boys are out. Is that understood?" Jabez said firmly.

"Well—I can't say I exactly understand it. But—" Zena sighed. Saying goodbye to a horde of strange boys, before she had had a chance to say hello, did seem extreme.

Jabez, reading her mind, said, gently for him, "It will be worth it."

Zena looked at this strange man, who was himself the stranger, as she had never before looked at anyone. Here was a best friend who was the keeper of her whole future. "It will be worth it," he had said. True, he had not added, "I promise." But looking at him with her heart more than with her eyes, she saw the promise, bright and clear.

Oh, Jabez, she wanted to say, you may not be what is called lovable, but I, Zena, do so love you.

Instead, she extended a hand as if it held her life and said, "Oh, sir, I do believe you."

If Jabez was touched by this absolute faith, he did not show it.

"But, sir—how did you come to make the mistake about knighting?"

"We are none of us perfect. Not even Jabez is. I was indulging in a daydream, a daydream of revenge, the most dangerous kind of daydream—when presto! before I knew it—"

"*Revenge?* Ooh. I don't understand—"

"You're not supposed to. Yet."

Jabez having almost thawed, now resumed his glacial chill.

"I did not intend to hear from you this soon," he said.

"Me either," Zena responded, eager to agree.

"Well then?"

"Well—"

"I am an extremely busy man. At this very moment three of the royal houses of Europe are urgently in need of my good offices, but not even I can be everywhere at once. I trust your need is greater than theirs?"

"Oh, it isn't my need. It's a friend's."

"A friend's? A *friend's?* I see I did not make myself clear. I am *not* community property. Far from it. I am a very exclusive matchmaker, excluding all but a select few as my clients. I do not have my card engraved by the gross to be handed out on street corners like a fortune teller's or a Reader and Adviser's. I am not in the habit of looking for clients. Quite the contrary."

"But Jabez you *did* hand me your card, and it was—"

"*You* happen to be the exception that proves my rule. I regret to inform you that you have now used up one of your chances."

"One of my chances? What do you mean?"

"Exactly what I say. The card is now blank, is it not?"

Zena was stunned. "Absolutely blank. You mean it won't work again?"

"Certainly not."

"Oh! Oh, that's not fair—I mean you never said— please, Jabez, how many chances do I get?"

"Since I am a man of many moods, the answer to that question is chancy, on which note we will close that subject."

"Oh, sir, please—if I promise never ever—"

"Closed. When I close a subject, it stays closed. The subject of chances is closed."

"Y-yes, sir."

It crossed Zena's mind that Jabez was the moodiest best friend she had ever had.

It was getting darker and colder in the park, and she shivered. So did the cat whose fur stood up in menacing spikes.

"I apologize, Jabez, for taking you away from all those kings and queens," she said. "And I do hope I have not ruined my whole life . . . ?"

Jabez chose not to answer.

Zena sighed.

Jabez waited.

Zena sighed again.

"Poor Bernice. My poor friend Bernice. I did think you were the one and only person in the whole world who could have helped her."

"I am immune to flattery."

"Well then . . . maybe not even you could have come to her rescue?"

"I am immune to tricks."

"Bernice's mama says Bernice is a hopeless case."

"There is no such thing."

"Not even if the person is more interested in warblers than in husbands?"

"Warblers?"

"A myrtle warbler most of all."

"A *myrtle* warbler? Eh? Arrives late in September.

One of the confusing fall warblers. Leaves early in May. Overwinters here. It is now winter. Nothing hopeless about it. Difficult? Yes. Tricky? Yes. Hopeless? No."

"Excuse me, Jabez, but I'm not following you."

"You weren't meant to. What you have just heard was an artist at work. No one understands that. Least of all the artist himself. You see, my dear, the shortest distance between two points may be a straight line, but a straight line is not always the recommended path to a husband."

"I'm sure Bernice would be happy to zigzag all over the place, if only she knew how, if only there was someone someplace to show her the way. Are you sure she isn't hopeless?"

Jabez drew himself up. "I see you have forgotten who I am."

"Oh, I would never do a thing like that. Never. I only—"

"You only are incurably curious. Impatient, too. Always turning to the back of the book to see how it ends, eh?"

Zena admitted to that deplorable weakness.

"I am impossible to fool. I was not born yesterday." He smiled icily. "No. Not yesterday, nor the day before either. You wish to see Jabez at work? I do not blame you. It is well worth seeing. Come with your warbler friend. Tomorrow. Same time. Same place."

"Oh, thank you, thank you."

Jabez raised his hand. "Enough! I do not seek your gratitude. To be honest, I, too, am curious. To be sure,

72

mine is the curiosity of an artist. You see, so far I have not been called upon to make a match for one who has lost her heart to a myrtle warbler. Who knows? It may prove amusing. So then—farewell—until tomorrow."

He pointed toward the path.

She waited for him to join her, but he waved her on impatiently.

She had only gone a few yards, when she wondered what she was to do if Bernice were busy tomorrow. She turned to ask Jabez, but he had disappeared. There was not a sign of him to be seen. The cat had disappeared too.

Mauve was deepening to purple. The castle towered above, lonely and secretive. Zena hurried home through the park.

Bernice *was* busy. She was truly sorry that she could not meet Zena's friend, the one who would be able to help her, but unfortunately she did have a previous engagement. Had Zena gone to much trouble?

Trouble? Zena smiled; sweetly she hoped. "Bernice —Bernice, to be absolutely frank, my friend is not exactly a cinch to get hold of. Bernice, you can break your previous engagement, can't you?"

Bernice shook her head. "Oh, I shouldn't. You see, a friend is counting on me to bird watch with her. Besides, it's the time of the migration and who knows? At long last I might see a myrtle warbler."

Zena felt a most unexpected surge of sympathy for Bernice's hysterical mother.

"Bernice," she said impatiently, "what's so great about a myrtle warbler anyhow?"

"Why, Zena, to tell the truth I don't know. I've never seen one. That's the whole point. It's the mystery of it. You see warblers are difficult. Of course if I went where the bayberry grows—"

"*Bayberry?*" Zena shrieked.

Bernice stepped back in alarm. "Goodness! What's the matter with bayberry? That's where the myrtles are."

Zena pulled herself together. "Nothing. Not a thing in the world. It just took me by surprise, that's all. I mean it does seem like a funny place to have to go to see a bird. But, and it really and truly is an *enormous* but, it makes me positive that you certainly better see *my* friend instead of *your* friend. Don't ask me to explain, just take my word for it. Bernice, it could be your last chance, your one and only last chance."

It was then that Zena realized that Jabez had not given her another card, that she had no way of reaching him to call off the meeting. If she pulled him away from kings and queens again, that would surely finish her with him.

"Bernice," she said as pathetically as she could, "you don't want to ruin *both* our lives, do you?"

Poor Bernice was thoroughly bewildered, but as kind hearted as ever. "Oh, I wouldn't want to do that," she said.

"Thank heaven!" Zena said. She dropped her voice, "The castle. Tomorrow at dusk."

74

Bernice drew her breath in. She had the terrified and embarrassed look of a large animal caught in a small trap.

The cold and the wind were fierce as Zena and Bernice hurried toward the dark towers of the castle. Zena thought with longing of her cozy room where she could now be curled up in the cushions of a window seat, reading a blood curdling mystery and feeling sorry for everyone who had the misfortune to be out in this cold and this wind. She could now be there, if she were not being a good samaritan.

"Have you known your friend long?" Bernice asked, although to talk in this wind was difficult and painful.

"Long enough," Zena shouted back.

Zena avoided looking at Bernice. Bernice was wearing her Sunday coat and hat. For some reason, Bernice's having got all dressed up to meet Jabez made her pathetic. It saddened Zena, and made her uneasy too because Bernice's Sunday clothes were not nearly so becoming as her sturdy bird watching mackintosh. Zena hoped that dusk would gather speed as it fell.

"What is your friend's name?"

"Jabez."

"Jabez? Jabez what?"

"Jabez nothing. Just Jabez."

"Oh."

Bernice pulled the squirrel collar of her best coat closer.

This time Jabez was waiting. Jabez and the cat. Sil-

75

houetted against the austere castle, they were planted on the snow like two black statues impervious not only to the cold and the wind, but to time itself.

At the sight of them, Bernice stumbled and came to a dead stop.

"Come on," Zena urged her on in a whisper. "Jabez is a very busy man."

Having just recently been drilled by Aunt Cassandra in the etiquette of the formal introduction, Zena decided that, if ever there was one, this must be an appropriate occasion for using it.

"May I have the honor of presenting," she shouted against the wind. Then she stopped. Jabez wasn't listening; he was too busy appraising Bernice, judging her with his eyes squinted, as if she were a horse.

Not by so much as the flicker of an eyelash, did Jabez divulge the result of this appraisal.

"Now then," he said. "I understand that you have been afflicted by an all consuming desire to see the myrtle warbler?"

"Um—ah—um—"

"In which case—" He reached into his coat pocket and brought out a small pair of mother of pearl opera glasses and handed them to Bernice with a flourish.

"But—but—" Bernice stammered.

Once again Jabez reached into his pocket. This time, when his hand came out it was cupped. He twisted his hand toward Bernice, and, there, peering out from the grey doeskin glove was the head of a tiny bird.

"Oh—oh—oh—"

Jabez opened his hand. The bird sat on his palm, rocking in the wind. It was a tiny, brownish, most undistinguished looking bird.

"The yellow rump—" Bernice cried hoarsely, "the yellow rump—"

The bird fluttered its wings. In the next second, it took flight.

With the dexterity of the expert, Bernice trained the glasses on the speck heading south in the darkening sky.

"You have now seen the myrtle warbler. Is that or is it not true?"

Bernice's eyes were shining with tears. "T-t-true."

"So be it. Now, now we can get down to business. Follow me."

"But how—but where did it come from?" Bernice called out.

"I have my sources," Jabez replied over his shoulder.

The wind was whistling and roaring through the park as they followed Jabez and the cat. Bernice, appearing to be in a trance, chanted, "I have seen it, I have seen it, I have seen the myrtle warbler."

On a bend in the road, the black electric stood waiting, with a mysterious, secret life of its own. Jabez went directly toward it and motioned them to follow.

"Where are we going?" Bernice, frightened, asked Zena.

"How should I know?"

"But we have to be home in time for dinner."

"Sh-h-h! Do you want a husband or don't you?"

"I—I don't know."

"Bernice!" Zena was losing patience.

"Yes—all right, yes, I do."

"In that case—"

Zena gave Bernice a shove toward the electric.

Jabez opened the door and Zena stepped onto the running board, which was lower than most other boards because this was an automobile favored by ladies.

It was a blessing to be out of the cold and the wind. The interior was soft as velvet, and when Jabez flicked the light on, there, in the crystal vase was the yellow rose, seeming to have the morning dew still on it.

Bernice and Zena sat close together on the back seat, and Jabez sat facing them on the jump seat. The cat sat on the floor next to him. Jabez opened a small leather book and made some notes rapidly with a gold pencil.

"Now then. Your name—"

"Bernice."

"Age?"

"Nineteen."

"Not a minute too soon," Jabez said as he continued to make notes.

At last! This was it, where it would all begin. Zena sat on the edge of the seat intent on memorizing the magic words that Jabez would utter.

"Height?"

"Oh, dear. Five feet eight and three-quarter inches, I'm afraid."

Jabez grunted.

In those days, before vitamins were all the rage, that

was considered to be a height better suited to a giraffe than a girl. Thank goodness, Zena thought, so far she was rather small for her age, a handicap when playing basketball but apparently an asset when seeking a husband.

"French?" Jabez shot the question at Bernice.

"I do beg your pardon?"

"*Parlez-vous français?* Do you or do you not speak French?"

"Not very well I'm afraid."

"Improve. It would help if I could present you as a young lady a gentleman could count on to translate a French menu, give orders to a steward on the *Ile de France*, or trade insults with a Parisian cab driver."

"Insults? Oh, sir, I don't think—"

Zena gave Bernice a brisk kick on her shin.

Bernice winced. "Very well, sir."

"Piano?"

"No sir."

"No sir? You have no piano? You cannot play the piano? Not even *The Happy Farmer?*"

"No sir. But I can play *Chopsticks.*"

Jabez let the gold pencil slip from his fingers. It fell to the floor, and Zena was quick to pick it up.

"Please?" she coaxed Jabez as she handed him the pencil.

He sighed heavily, then he addressed Bernice:

"My dear young lady, it would be a matter of the greatest importance if you were to replace *Chopsticks* with a more appropriate composition, preferably with a

79

little Liszt, a little Chopin. Believe me, my dear young lady, this is no idle suggestion. You see, music has great powers. It is well known that it has the power to soothe a savage breast, soften a rock, etcetera, etcetera. To be perfectly blunt about it, we may be in need of that power." Then, out of a belated regard for Bernice's feelings, he looked away from her and went on, speaking softly, "Yes, music transforms . . . transports . . ."

Jabez's lids drooped and he began to hum. As might be expected, his was no ordinary singing voice; it was harsh and yet underneath there was the haunting sound of an ancient instrument too long silent. But the melody was true, and the cat rubbed against his leg and purred and the wind, which had been violent enough to rock the electric, died down.

As he hummed, Jabez swayed to the music and waved an imaginary baton.

"What am I singing?" He stopped abruptly to ask Bernice.

"Um—ah—" Bernice stammered nervously.

"Ah-h-h . . ." Zena sighed ecstatically.

"Yes?" Jabez prodded.

"A little Liszt, a little Chopin?" Zena guessed.

"Correct. Now we will do a little experiment in the interest of science—and philosophy, *my* philosophy. I will sing once more and you will describe what happens to you when you hear this music. So . . ."

A little Liszt, a little Chopin . . . Zena too began to sway to the music that filled the electric with its sweet nostalgia crackled by the roughness of Jabez's voice.

"So?" Jabez asked.

Zena took a big breath. "Ooh. I—I was in a ballroom, an ivory one. And there were chandeliers, enormous crystal ones. And underneath them there was me, me, Zena, in yards and yards of chiffon, floating and waltzing . . . waltzing . . . mmn . . . waltzing . . . lovely, oh, it was lovely . . ."

"That will do. No raving please. Now then. According to your Webster chap, that which you have just described is called being transported. You agree that you were transported?"

"Oh, I certainly do."

"However, I must remind you that in fact you never left this electric." He paused dramatically. "According to *me*, an expert on the subject, that which you have just experienced was an illusion, a charming one, was it not?"

"Oh, very."

"It was of the sort *I* call the true illusions—to distinguish them from the false ones your flappers live by. The true illusion is not to be had from a flask of wretched bootleg liquor, but from those other spirits— the artists, if you please, the musicians, the writers, the painters, etcetera, etcetera. And from me, in a manner of speaking. It is the illusion that is to be had from one's own wit and imagination. And if one does not possess these, one should borrow them—from one's betters. Yes, I am very fond of these illusions. They often make that which is unbearable, bearable and that which is pleasant, more pleasant. Though they belong to the pleasures of life, these illusions do not leave one with a splitting headache and the wish to be dead, with what I believe is called a hangover. These illusions . . ." The cat stretched and yawned noisily. Jabez spoke to him, sarcastically. "So sorry I'm boring you. What if you have heard this all a hundred times before? They all have to be told. Secretly they all want to be flappers, brave flappers fighting for freedom they think . . ." The cat pawed the air impatiently. ". . . little do they know, these flappers, that they are the symptoms who mistake themselves for the cure. These poor flappers . . ." the cat slapped Jabez, hard, ". . . what's that? Oh, yes. Piano playing . . ."

The cat sighed and went to sleep.

"As I was saying, it is an important aid. And even an artist such as I am, can use a little assistance from his subject in the creation of the true illusion. Is not that so?"

Yes, yes, Bernice and Zena chorused, alto. Good, good, Jabez responded, basso. The cat woke up and meowed.

But what about pianos that were so important, Zena wondered? How would she ever wangle one out of her mama, who did not believe in spoiling people? Would Mama think they were good for children or bad for children? There was no telling.

Jabez closed his little book and put it away.

Without warning, coming from some distant disturbance in the heavens, there was a great clap of thunder.

Thunder in the winter, out of season.

Silently, Jabez flipped the light off, set the electric in motion and silently, they went skimming over the snow covered road.

"Oh . . . oh, where are we going now?" Bernice whispered.

"Just for a little ride," Jabez apparently heard everything.

There was another great clap of thunder.

"Oh, the poor little warbler," Bernice moaned.

"Yes, the poor little warbler," Zena echoed.

They skimmed past the lake, the dark rush of trees, lights flickering palely in the old lamp posts, the Sheep Meadow. They went past the Bethesda Fountain where two old ladies were walking their dogs. They came to a stop opposite the blazing Plaza. There the bank of horse drawn hansoms waited to take persons romantically or nostalgically or scenically inclined for a slow trot through the snowy park.

The blanket covered horses were steaming the cold air with their breath and the huddle of top-hatted coachmen were stamping their feet and thumping their chests to keep warm. At the sight of the black electric, as one man, the coachmen tipped their hats. And the horses? The horses dipped their heads and delicately pawed once.

"Did you see that? Isn't Jabez a wonder?" Zena whispered triumphantly into Bernice's ear.

"I—I think so," Bernice whispered back.

"You did so see it," Zena whispered. "You did."

"Take her word for it," Jabez said out loud.

83

Jabez spun the electric around and went back into the park retracing their way, until he came to the exit directly opposite the many-gabled house. There he stopped and opened the door.

Bernice hopped out as quickly as she could.

"Remember," Jabez said to her, "remember all that you heard, all that you saw, remember a little Liszt, a little Chopin never hurt anyone. You will be hearing from me."

"Yes—yes, sir."

"And as for you," Jabez said to Zena, who lingered, "for you there is another chance."

And Jabez slipped a card into Zena's hand.

"Oh, thank you, thank you so much."

If Jabez had not ducked, Zena might very well have kissed him on the cheek.

CHAPTER 8

THAT SEASON WAS BRIGHT with questions dancing in and out of the winter days like sunbeams. When would Jabez conjure up Bernice's Own True Love? And where? And how? And, incidentally, who would he turn out to be?

Vera reported curious doings. Bernice was not herself. One morning, without any explanation, she moved her precious bird books to a shelf way out of reach. In their place, had come Chardenal's French Course, Conversational French, books on the cuisine of France and, of all things, the tales of Monsieur Grimm and Monsieur Anderson, in French. Wasn't Bernice really too old for fairy tales in any language? And at dinner, there she was, always struggling to give the food their French names. One night, when she had wondered what the French was for the German meatball called Koenigsberger Klops, the waitress had laughed so hard she dropped the platter and was fired, not for sending Klops all over the dining room floor, but for having made Bernice nervous about her ambition to educate herself.

A strangeness had come over their mama too, Vera reported. She seemed to be holding her breath all the time. No one was allowed to say boo to Bernice. It was as if Bernice were under a spell, and Mama was determined to have her jolly well stay under.

What, Vera wondered, did Zena think was going on?

Something mysterious no doubt, Zena ventured, crossing her fingers as she did so.

Naturally, it was Bernice herself that Zena most wanted to hear from. But Bernice appeared to be avoiding her. All that Zena had been able to extract from her was that yes, she was in touch with you-know-who, but not where or how or to what end. Hopefully, Zena supposed that it was another case of the less said the better.

However, one day when she met Bernice coming out of the park wearing her binoculars, Zena's heart sank. As well it might. That day Bernice talked.

Anyone, Bernice said, but *anyone* can make a mistake. For instance, it is a mistake to introduce a suitor, who is already engaged to one lady, to another lady who is in need of a suitor herself, is it not? After considering this muddle, Zena nodded.

But if she, Bernice, lived to be three million years old there was one kind of suitor she could never, never learn to love. And what kind of suitor could that possibly be? Zena inquired. The kind of suitor, Bernice said sternly, who devotes himself to hunting the beautiful wild duck of Maryland, the dear little quail of Virginia, and travels as far away as Scotland to kill an innocent grouse that never harmed anyone.

Zena acknowledged that for a bird lover like Bernice that was a bit of mismatching. Jabez must have been sorry to have made such a mistake?

No, not really. On the contrary, if the truth must be told, he had been annoyed and had said haughtily, "So. The field is now narrowed to exclude gentlemen of noble birth where I have the best connections. So be it."

Bernice went on to say that since she honestly did not aspire to princes the way so many girls she knew did, that didn't bother her the least bit but . . . but had Jabez come well recommended? That is to say, to put it bluntly, did Jabez really know his business?

Good Lord! Does the north wind know its business? Zena wanted to ask. Does summer rain? For that matter, a bolt of lightning? What kind of question was that? She said none of it, because Bernice might with good reason ask her to explain the connection. She couldn't. And wouldn't, if she could. It was her opinion that, once again, the less explained the better. But it was the truth she spoke when she said, "I feel that Jabez knows his business, Bernice. And if I were you, I would feel likewise."

Bernice agreed to try.

And Zena decided not to worry. Her faith in Jabez was not shaken. The course of true love, Shakespeare said, never did run smooth. And she imagined that he knew what he was talking about. But why true love should have a bumpier time of it than untrue love was beyond her; and for all she knew, it was beyond Shakespeare too.

Her own way was to have its own obstacles.

For instance, there was Mama. Mama was a mysterious lady, but her reaction to Zena's courteous, humble, earnest, in every way unexceptionable, request for piano lessons was too mysterious even for Mama.

You would have thought that learning to play the piano had been recommended by the devil himself.

"What's this? What's this?" Mama asked, herself breathing fire. Then her black eyes had veiled, and she had asked: "Zena, the truth. Have you been talking to— to strangers?"

"Mama!" The shock in Zena's voice had been genuine enough, but not for the reason Mama might think. Mama was internationally famous for being smart, but was she also clairvoyant?

"Goodness," Zena had replied, "what do strangers have to do with pianos?"

Mama hadn't answered, but the next thing Zena knew the Tribunal went into session. That usually meant trouble for Zena. This time the whispering behind closed doors hissed like a witch's brew. "But Augusta, playing the piano is both ladylike *and* educational, a rare combination." Zena, whose ears were acutely sensitive to voices behind closed doors, heard Benedicta say, "And, Augusta dear, I do believe it encourages cleanliness. Must not one always wash one's hands before touching the ivory keys?"

Poor Benedicta had not quite finished her question when the door shook and bric-a-brac rattled as something hit the floor with a great thump. Zena knew that something was Mama's slender foot coming down like a sledge hammer.

"Geese!" Mama shouted. "There will be no pianos in this house now—or ever! Absolutely no pianos!"

Zena was flabbergasted. Zena was used to flabbergastation, it being the normal condition when living with grown-ups. But she was not used to having what was after all a noble request bring on such a temper tantrum, nor was she used to having Benedicta and Cassandra on her side. Usually, they were much more worried about her being spoiled than Mama was.

She planned to put this problem in Jabez's hands at the first opportunity, but she had no intention of wasting a precious chance on a piano.

Besides, there were one or two other matters on her mind in addition to love.

For instance, was she pretty?

A M I PRETTY?"

In the house of clocks, looking glasses were scarce. There were two. A full length mahogany framed cheval glass in Mama's room, and one painted white in Zena's. Their purpose was strictly utilitarian—straight hems, straight stocking seams, buttons buttoned, sashes tied, each and every hair in its proper place.

The white looking glass did confirm that one had yellow hair and that green was the true color of one's eyes, blue coming on with sadness and black with anger. Grimacing like an idiot, one was presented with a set of strong white teeth. And standing naked, from top to bottom there were no visible deformities, not even any interesting birth marks, nothing but pinkish-white skin. But what did all these colors add up to? A rainbow? Or a ragbag?

"Am I pretty?" Zena had asked Crystal.

"Dead from pneumonia you'll be with such vanity." Crystal had hastily wrapped her in a comforter, turning her into a cocoon. "The answer to that question is in the eyes of the beholder, ducky."

As for beholders, as Zena traveled about the city, it was not long before various people from various places claimed her as their own. "Ah," exclaimed the French, "*regardez cette fille. Made in France, n'est-ce pas? Vive la France!*" And the Italians said it in Italian. And the Greeks in Greek. And the Scandinavians in Scandinavian. And so it went. She was internationally popular with strangers.

But not with the mothers of daughters, not with the daughters themselves.

It had to do with boys. At the parties of her classmates, through no fault of her own—pretty or not—the minute Zena entered a room, it would happen: If boys were talking, they would forget what they were saying; if they were eating, they would lose their appetite; if they were dancing, they would step on their partners' feet. Zena really did make a mess of a girl's party.

"What do you do?" Vera, who had remained loyal, would ask plaintively.

"Nothing," Zena would answer honestly and as bewildered as anyone.

Could it be that boys *sensed* that she had the power to knight? She had been good about that: Since Jabez asked her not to, she had not knighted a single person, although it took a great deal of effort and concentration not to. (Once or twice she had had an accident and knighted someone in spite of herself.)

"And you're not even a flapper," Vera said. "It's very puzzling. Only flappers are supposed to be *that* popular."

No, Zena had not become a flapper. Yes, there were those secret longings to be one. But there was an intuitive reason for not becoming one, a reason beyond Jabez's aversion to them—or what would have been the Mamas' horror—a reason that stirred at her center. Vaguely, it had to do with flappers being boyish and her being girlish.

Being popular with boys and not with girls sometime made one lonely. So did waiting for one's Own True Love. One went to parties and danced with boys, but dates of course were forbidden. "Strange boys are out!" Jabez had decreed—and so had Mama for that matter. (So, in a way, had many mamas in those days; early dating, in those days, was not all the rage it was to become—except with flappers.) But a little loneliness now and then was not so awful, if one had a Jabez to count on, a Jabez who was to conjure up One's Own True Love.

In the next year or so, time played its customary tricks: Zena grew older; Zena grew younger; and there were times when she wondered how anyone ever got to be the right age at the right time.

She also wondered when Jabez was ever going to make that match for Bernice.

One day, just as she was wondering about this, Jabez appeared.

It was another of those very windy days, and she was walking along Central Park West, wondering, when her hat went kiting into the gutter.

A young man, in a crimson sweater, coming out of the park caught sight first of yellow hair blowing about, then green eyes. He glanced at these, frowning, then he made a leap for the hat, directly into the path of an oncoming ice wagon. The driver reined in the horse and cursed furiously.

"It's you again!" he shouted to Zena. "I remember you from back there. Always giving my horse apoplexy. You'll kill him one of these days if you don't mind what you're doing. You just stop doing whatever you're doing. Do you hear me?"

Before Zena could say a word in her own defense, the young man had many words to say to the ice man, all angry ones, all in her defense. The crimson sweater having been modestly turned inside out, she could nevertheless see the outline of the H and was not surprised at this young man's bravery.

Out of a sincere desire to show her appreciation—and with a sense that this was a most fitting moment to do so—Zena could not resist knighting this young man. She smiled a certain smile, and she looked a certain look.

Nothing happened. The young man remained exactly as he was—quite at his ease as he studied Zena.

Goodness gracious! she thought, have I lost the power so soon? Just when before long I may need it most, to knight my Own True Love? It was an unsettling thought.

Once again she smiled a certain smile and looked a certain look. And this time, it must be admitted, she gave it all she had.

And still nothing happened!

"You aren't by any chance practising to be the Mona Lisa, are you?" the young man asked.

Zena withdrew the smile and the look and replaced it with a scowl.

"And do you still hang out of windows upside down?" he continued.

It was then that Zena noticed the ragged crest of hair.

"It's you again!"

They said it together, he mocking her.

"But why——" But why aren't you knightable? she longed to ask.

"Because——" the young man began, as if he had read her mind.

That was as far as he got when the black electric pulled up.

Jabez and the cat jumped out. Jabez glared. The ice man (who had been alternately muttering and growling) said "Giddap!" and moved on.

The young man, still clutching Zena's hat, undaunted, stared at Jabez. And Jabez, more frightening than Zena had ever before seen him, not only glared at this young man but breathed fire, too.

Quite clearly, this was a young man who did not give up easily. His eyes went back and forth from Jabez to Zena, back and forth. When he saw the cat with its back up and its teeth bared, he gave up, not easily however; and handed the hat to Zena.

"I see . . ." the young man said sadly.

"But thank you so much anyhow," said Zena,

strangely sad herself.

Zena watched the young man walk away. For some reason, he went back into the park. Just before he disappeared, he raised his hand. Was it a salute or a warning?

"Come, come." Jabez urged Zena toward the electric.

Zena wasn't listening.

"But Jabez—I *couldn't* knight him."

Jabez came to a dead stop.

"What did you say?"

"I said I couldn't knight him. I tried as hard as I could and I couldn't."

"Didn't I tell you to stop doing that—until the time came?" Jabez asked angrily. "Didn't I tell you strangers were *out?*"

"I know, but Jabez he was *so* brave, just the kind to be knighted. Jabez, did you take the power away from me?"

"I did no such thing." Jabez looked around rather wildly. He dropped his voice. "Here, quick! See if you can knight this good-for-nothing playboy—"

The playboy, a dapper fashion plate, was sauntering down the avenue twirling his slender walking stick and wondering which of six cocktail parties he would attend.

"But I thought—" Zena began.

"Don't argue. Quick! Strictly in the interest of science."

Zena smiled the smile and looked the look.

The playboy's hand went to his shoulder and the walking stick became a sword. He was knighted all right. (Indeed, he went to no cocktail party that afternoon, but straight to the Museum of Natural History where he began a study of fauna and flora that was to make him a world famous naturalist.)

"Goodness gracious!" Zena exclaimed. "I don't understand it. Do you?"

Jabez was deep in thought. "No, I don't. But I can tell you one thing, I don't like it, not one bit. Come, come, get into the electric. Clearly, the time has come for a little chat."

As Zena sat down on the jump seat facing Jabez, she felt a shiver of excitement. Has the time come?

She had not however, forgotten the brave young man with the H on his sweater. Far from it. (Nor would she. Every once in a while, when least expected, she would remember a ragged crest of black hair and a hand raised —in salute or warning?)

"Jabez, do you know you were just rude to a Harvard man?"

"You don't say. As for Harvard," Jabez said, as he headed the electric into the park, "the very name sends me to my pillbox."

So saying, he opened a little eighteenth century enamel pillbox and from a spectrum of pills plucked a crimson one.

"The Harvard pill. And a bitter one it is to swallow. On the Eastern seaboard of the United States of America, there is a widely accepted superstition that the most suitable suitors are Harvard men. The energy required to combat this idiotic superstition raises my blood pressure." Jabez swallowed the pill and shuddered. "For such as you, there may or may not be a Harvard man, just as for such as you there may be one who never so much as set foot in a university—and I am including Oxford and Cambridge—England, of course —but one who was privately tutored by renowned specialists. I am referring of course to the crowned princes of Europe."

"Mmn," Zena murmured.

"Bearing that in mind, in the future you will kindly hang on to your hat." Jabez was being icily polite.

"But it's very, very windy out there."

"Precisely. I suggest that you hang on to your hat even in the face of a hurricane. I will not have you knighting every Tom, Dick, and Harry. As I told you before, in the end it will be Jabez who will present *the* knight, only Jabez, no one else. For if it is not I who am to present him, then we may as well call it quits now, is not that so?"

"Y-yes, Jabez. I mean no, Jabez, no. Oh, please don't call it quits, please."

"Then kindly say, 'Yes, Jabez' with more conviction."

"*Yes*, Jabez."

"That's better. However, I still detect a disturbance. Out with it!"

"It's about Bernice. Please, sir, what's happening to Bernice?"

"Instant magic is not my forte," Jabez said. "That sort of abracadabra nonsense is for vaudevillians who produce rabbits, not husbands."

They drove through a cloud of falling leaves. The sheep grazing on Sheep Meadow stopped long enough

97

to stare at the black electric with the red-haired man and the yellow-haired girl. Before they went back to their grazing, they let out a long, low "Baa-a-a!" On their way into the Casino for tea, five college men escorting three flappers turned to stare. The flappers glared.

"Yes," said Jabez, "it is time for a little chat."

"Mmn," Zena murmured, expectantly.

"To begin with, *parlez-vous français?*"

"*Oui, monsieur.* You mean—I'm old enough *already?*" Zena asked.

"Certainly not. But you are old enough to begin to acquire the necessary charming graces. One does not learn a little Liszt, a little Chopin overnight, does one?"

"Not unless one is a musical genius, I suppose."

"Which I take it you are not. Therefore, I propose that you begin now."

"Oh, Jabez, is that absolutely necessary?"

"*Necessary?* With you one does not speak of necessities, one speaks of," he glanced at the yellow rose in the vase, "one speaks of providing the appropriate vessel, so to speak."

"Well, that vessel will just have to do without Liszt and Chopin."

"I beg your pardon?"

"Mama says no pianos, absolutely *no pianos.* And when Mama says no, there isn't any maybe to it. Oh, Jabez . . ."

"You asked for a piano?"

"Oh, I did. After listening to what you had to say to Bernice. Mama was furious. Exceptionally furious."

"She was, was she?"

"She certainly was. The Mamas had a whole meeting about it."

"They did, did they?"

"They did. Now what am I going to do?"

"*You* are going to do nothing. But I must say, you did act precociously, that is, before your time. In the future, you will kindly wait for instructions from me."

"Yes, Jabez. Oh, Jabez, have I already ruined it for myself?"

Jabez refused to answer.

"Tell me," he asked, "did your mama stamp her foot?"

"She did. But guess who was on my side?"

"The other two. Geese!"

"Why, Jabez, that's just what Mama called them." She looked at Jabez. "Do you know Mama?"

"In my profession, one gets to know *genus mama* as one gets to know the palm of one's hand. What exactly did your excessively—um—intemperate mama say?"

"She said, 'There will be no pianos in this house now—or ever! No pianos!'" Zena mimed her mama well.

Jabez threw his head back and laughed. The laugh was the sort that is more menacing than mirthful.

"No pianos, eh? Well, we'll see about that."

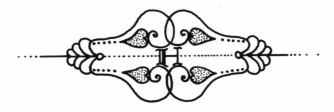

CHAPTER 10

N O SOONER SAID than done.

It so happened that the next day was an ordinary Tuesday. Tuesday is quite the most ordinary day of the week and hence nothing much is expected of it. So, when Zena came home from school, her first thought was that she was not home at all, but had entered the house of a stranger. But there they were, the gods of this household, the clocks, standing as always. However, their ticking was not to be heard. For floating, swirling, rising, falling, in lovely trills and glissandos, dappling the dark forest with sunlight, was the sound of music, the sound of a *piano*.

Zena stood still in her disbelief, her books spilling out of her arms on to the floor. Then she flew toward the music.

At the room at last come into its own, the music

room, she skidded to a stop.

Where only yesterday, there had been potted palms and aspidistras filling a void, there was now a curving mass of shining ebony. It was nothing less than the most beautiful piano in the world.

The music stopped abruptly.

"You—you are the pupil?" a catarrhal voice asked, as if this were beyond belief.

"Oh, I am! I am! I am! And you—?" Zena's smile was dazzling.

A shadowy man, neither young nor old, rose from the piano stool as if he were being levitated.

"Professor Schmidt here. The—the teacher." As if proof were needed to convince himself more than anyone else, he presented his card.

"You mean my mama, *my* mama changed her mind?"

He fluttered a pale, delicate hand. "Please! Please! I know nothing. I know only I have my orders."

"And they are for—a little Liszt, a little Chopin?"

A shadow crossed Professor Schmidt's shadowy face.

"I have my orders. Always it is a little Liszt, a little Chopin. But one day—one day my great wish is that the order will be for Bach." His voice had dropped to a reverent hush. He shook himself. "Ach! I forget myself. Let us now please to begin—"

Professor Schmidt was never to forget that beginning.

Until that moment, it had been Professor Schmidt's unhappy lot to teach tone deaf, unmusical young girls who regarded their weekly hour with him as something to be endured, like having their teeth straightened. To have this one with the yellow hair and the green eyes—as unmusical as the rest, he could see—greet his presence with a warmth, a happiness that outdid his dear doting mother, gave him vertigo. To have her hang on his words as if her life depended on them, to have her watch his fingers on the keyboard as if they held a rare and precious secret, frightened him. He asked for aspirin and a glass of water.

Professor Schmidt walked away from the many-gabled house in a daze. Always when he left his pupils, he immediately filled his head with Bach, letting the music wash away his misery. Professor Schmidt lived by the side of the great fugues as if they were the sea. Now his head was filled with two questions fighting each other. Was he to be the victim of a new plot to bedevil the life of a poor piano teacher? Or—or—with second sight in those green eyes had this creature discovered some hidden charm in him, one that had escaped even his dear mother? Torn between these two extremes, Professor Schmidt for once in his life indulged himself and inclined toward the happier prospect.

Before Mama barely had one foot in the front door, Zena rushed toward her.

"Thank you, Mama, thank you with all my heart."

Mama backed away.

"For what?"

"Mama! For *what?* For the piano of course."

Mama came as close to showing fear as Mama could.

Or was it anger? Or could it be both? Or neither? Then what was it if it was none of these?

Mama just stood there silently.

It wasn't as if Zena hadn't got used to Mama's odd—and delightful—way of giving gifts. Mama always disowned them. "Doll? What doll?" Mama would say of a new doll unexpectedly come to join the others, or "Bracelet? What bracelet?" of one suddenly appearing in Zena's bureau drawer. Mama acted as if giving people presents embarrassed her—or was it being thanked that did? Whatever it was, Mama was famous for being an anonymous donor.

But to deny a piano! That was too much. Zena detected secrets enclosed in secrets like Chinese boxes.

"Mama—?"

Before Zena could phrase the question, Crystal appeared, her head bandaged in her headache scarf doused in vinegar.

Crystal and Mama avoided each other's eyes.

"I have a headache, madam," Crystal said, as if that were not self-evident.

"I plan to use *my* head to better advantage," Mama said.

"I will pray for your success, madam," Crystal said, obviously anticipating failure.

Mama, who always walked like an Indian, now took an uncertain step.

"What's this all about?" Zena asked.

As if all at once she didn't know. She had never thought of herself as being psychic the way Mama was,

103

but if this wasn't all about Jabez she'd eat witches' broom.

And if she had not been stuck with a vow of secrecy, she would have told Mama and Crystal that she knew that much.

But how *did* they know Jabez?

And what did it *signify?*

"One day you will know," Mama said, as she swept out of the foyer.

Without turning around, Mama stopped and said, "One day you will know more than you care to."

I T W A S M A Y, and the hawthorns were in bloom.
In the spring the Irish in Crystal also bloomed,
bringing with it much talk of Little Folk and Spells and
People being carted off. What People? Carted off
where? Never mind. Crystal said May was a most
dangerous time for girls. Zena said she was starving for
some danger and went out for a stroll.

"Mind you don't eat those foolish words, you foolish
girl," Crystal called after her.

Inevitably, Zena found herself on the court of the castle. There, as usual, whatever was was more so—now
it was the sun that was sunnier and the breeze that was
breezier. Bewitched, she leaned over the parapet to
watch spring in Central Park. She saw a boy, all vanity,
ride his bicycle no hands; she saw the seesaw of a can-
tering white horse, a red kite tangle in the young leaves
of a maple, a rowboat drift on the lake, its oarsman

reading what must surely be poetry on such a day.

Presently, behind her she heard someone singing Liszt's *Liebestraum*, dream of love, singing it as if the dream had miraculously come true. Zena spun around, drawn to this voice as the flower is to the sun. "Bernice!"

Bernice ended on high *C*. The change in Bernice took Zena's breath away. The poorness had been peeled from her: eyes that had been doleful were now sparkling, skin that had been olive drab now glowed.

"Zena! Dear, dear Zena—"

"*Bernice! It's happened!*"

Bernice beamed. "How did you guess?" Bernice leaned over and kissed the top of Zena's head. "I wanted you to be the first to know. I owe it all to you."

"You mean Jabez."

"But it was you who introduced me to him."

"Who is it, Bernice? Tell me everything."

"I can do better than that."

"What do you mean?"

"You can meet him."

"Now?"

"This very minute. I saw you up here, and I had to come and tell you. Now follow me."

Bernice flew down the steps as if she could not bear to be parted one more minute from her Own True Love.

And flying after Bernice, Zena soared with the buoyancy that comes from happiness—and faith justified. In making this miraculous match for poor Bernice, Jabez had proved himself to be the great artist he claimed to be. Flying after Bernice, Zena soared with love for Jabez and love for Love.

"There he is!" Bernice called out.

His back was to them. He was walking in the Shakespeare Garden, beside the rosemary and the rue and the columbine. He was reading—poetry of course. What else on a day like this? At a time like this?

"Oh, Bernice," Zena murmured happily.

"Yoo-hoo," Bernice called in her hearty, outdoor way. Her betrothed, absorbed in his book, did not hear. Then he stopped, tilted his head skyward for a second and returned to the book, but this time to *write* in it. *Himself, the poet?*

"Ooh, Bernice!"

They were now only three or four yards away.

He turned. Zena froze.

There stood the *frog*. Ugly, *ugly frog*. Her instinct was to turn and run. With feet become weighted with despair, she forced herself to trail behind Bernice.

It was a short walk as the crow flies. But she was not a crow, she was a girl and it was a long, long walk that she took toward Bernice's Own True Love.

Do not judge the contents by the package. All that glitters is not gold. The proof of the pudding is in the eating. Fine feathers do not make fine birds. Beauty is only skin deep. Things are seldom what they seem, butter is oleomargarine.

The frog *did* turn into the prince. Didn't he?

"Dearest, this is Zena and Zena *this—this* is— Alban—"

He looked up from the book and acknowledged the introduction with an absentminded nod, the way a poet would.

Zena smiled at him. He did not return the smile.

He moistened his pencil with his tongue and wrote in his book. Then he smiled. At what he had written.

"Ah!" he said. "That does it. At six percent per annum on the savings to be had from the difference between the butt end and the flank end of a ham, the total in ten years will be . . ."

But Zena had stopped listening to him.

There was an awfulness happening inside her. She longed to lie down on the lovely new grass smelling of spring and romance, lie down beside the rosemary and the rue and howl like a baby.

"How clever you are, Alban dear," she heard Bernice gush, in a most un-Bernice-like way, as if this Alban had just invented relativity.

This Alban frog puffed with pride; almost—almost as if he had been knighted?

"Generally speaking, the average woman does not understand the *philosophy* of the budget. I always say that the penny saved today is tomorrow's dollar. If you should ever be in need of assistance—"

He opened a card case bursting with cards and handed one to Zena.

ALBAN KROOP

FINANCIER

Alban Kroop. Kroop. Kroop. The name of a child's disease. His name was too perfect, and Zena began to itch all over.

She mumbled something about being late (for what

she did not say) and left, holding the card by one corner as if it were a dead mouse.

She could barely see where she was going, and for all she knew spring had come and gone.

This was not the first time she had hated someone. In the second grade, she had hated Miss Drew—Drew, Drew full of glue, Drew, Drew's a rotten stew; in the fourth grade, there had been Pinky Moss—stinky Pinky's not my boss, death, death to Pinky Moss. Oh, there had been others, many others. With a heart like hers, so eager to love, so longing to love, you were bound to hate too. But she had never hated like this; this was a hate that made her giddy; this was a hate beyond stupid childish jingles; this hate was grown-up.

Then, snaking in to join the hate came an uglier feeling, the ugliest she had ever felt in her life.

She had been betrayed.

And Bernice, poor Bernice had been betrayed; Jabez had cast a spell over her, a dreadful, false one.

No, Jabez was not the Great Matchmaker; Jabez was the False Enchanter, the Great Traitor, Betrayer of Faith . . . of Love. The man who produced frogs, and called them True Loves.

She ran from the park so as not to weep in public.

CHAPTER 12

S HE RAN PAST DOORMEN and elevator men and neighbors, all of whom wondered what the trouble was. "That child's seen a ghost," one old lady said as if she knew what she was talking about. "Nonsense!" tinkled another lady, smugly corseted in middle age and in the habit of condescending to the young, "more likely disappointed in love. Ha! Ha!" She laughed archly, as if she had just made an adorable joke.

She ran past a parlormaid, a chambermaid, and a waitress, all of whom went running to Crystal with the news that the young miss was like to be having a fit about goodness only knows what.

Crystal, who was preparing spring lamb for the oven, cut her finger but paid it no heed. She went directly to Zena's room.

Zena, still not weeping, was curled up on the window seat, her face hidden by a curtain of yellow hair.

"I know all about it. I know what happened. I have my sources," Crystal said. "I warned you he was the enemy. You can't say I didn't. But you wouldn't listen, not you."

Zena covered her ears with her hands.

In a house where weeping was against the rules, Crystal was mopping her eyes.

For some minutes, Crystal stood there uncertainly, fidgeting and opening and closing her mouth, as if she had a secret that needed to be told. "Now?" she asked herself. No, she shook her head.

Instead, she said, softly, tentatively, "Ducky, ducky, I'm not saying it isn't hard to be young when it's all or nothing the heart will settle for—all or nothing. I'm not saying it isn't hard to lose all that innocent faith, so warm and lovely like baby fat. I'm not saying that. All I'm saying is that too much misery makes for—makes for—"

For once at a loss, Crystal left Zena alone, curled up on the window seat like a crumpled butterfly.

This time there was no light. This time it was the blackness of a cave she sought, not some moonlit gazebo. Feeling her way in the blackness, Zena struck a match and lit the bayberry candle. At once, she was assaulted by shadows that mocked and menaced as they did a frenzied war dance.

The card trembled in her hand. What if she was

using up her last chance to save Bernice? What of it? Who cared? It was good riddance to bad rubbish, wasn't it? Then why did she still have to feel so weepy? Because it's hard to be young . . . to lose faith? Or, a little voice whispered, because you are feeble-minded enough to hope that Jabez is still *your* friend? Idiot!

The question did not bring a flood of tears. Only a few large ones, made the more painful for having been held back, splashed on the card. (Holding back tears was using up a lot of bravery she had discovered.)

Would this card that was now tear stained work? Or ought she wait for it to dry? For another night perhaps?

The flame leapt forward as if to pull the card in.

"*J*—" she croaked, the letter sticking in her throat.

J is for Judas, that's what *J* is for.

The flame guttered furiously.

Quiet, quiet, all I want is to plead with you to please free Bernice from that ghastly spell.

She heard mocking laughter. So you wish Bernice to be set free from a spell that has taken the poorness out of poor Bernice. Oh, you do-gooders, what a tiresome breed you are, always insisting that the rest of the world be shaped in your own personal, self-centered, picayune image.

More laughter.

And then the flame began to die.

"Come back, come back," Zena called out, waving the card over it.

But the flame went out and once again the room was in total darkness.

Zena fumbled for the matches, struck one and held it

to the candle. The wick would not light.

"This is ridiculous," she said, striking another match, "absolutely ridiculous."

The candle still would not light.

Zena sat in the blackness clutching the card.

There would be some people practical minded enough to think that all that was needed was to buy a new candle.

Zena knew better. She knew it had happened, that the magic was gone, the magic inside her too.

In the darkness, she wept the most she ever had in her life.

When she stopped weeping, she realized that the card was no longer in her hand. Thinking she had dropped it, she turned on the light to find it. It had vanished.

All that remained of it was a smudge of ash on her hand.

No more card. No more Jabez.

Good. It was now official. Now she would never have to see him again as long as she lived; now she was spared the necessity of telling him exactly what she thought of him, of telling him that his services were no longer required.

That night she stood at her window seeing—and also not seeing—the dark park, the lights of the city, the lights of the Plaza. Trying not to weep again, she said her formal farewell to magic.

Just as she was about to leave the window, she saw a light she had never seen before, that didn't belong, that floated high above the dark shadows of the trees.

Straining to locate it, she saw that it could—it could

113

come from the tower of the castle.

This light, whatever it was, went on and off like a light warning of danger. Then it went out altogether.

Shivering, Zena ran to bed.

It was a warm spring night, but Zena pulled a comforter up to her chin. It was bone chilling to have one's whole life change so suddenly and to have one's future returned to one's own self on a cake of ice.

Zena lay there wide awake, thinking—or rather allowing her brain to spin like a rundown top, wobbling this way and that, backward and forward, from the happy, carefree past to the now uncertain, murky future.

It was while haphazardly meandering back to the time when she had guessed that Mama and Crystal knew Jabez, that she recalled Mama's saying, "One day you will know more than you care to."

Zena sat straight up in bed. Of course! Jabez must have been Mama's matchmaker too! Her *mis*matchmaker. Poor, poor Mama! No wonder she was so sad and so strange and so extra fearful of strangers. Oh yes, Jabez was the enemy, and he had not only put Mama under his spell and ruined Mama's life, but now he was about to ruin Bernice's too (thanks to her, Zena).

Zena thought about Mama with a love shot through with a new sympathy. Thinking about Mama, Zena supposed that way down inside of her she had guessed about Jabez and Mama; but having been such a fanatic about Jabez, she had pushed it back.

Well, that was then and now was now. And now she was alone, alone with her own future on her hands, and what was she going to do about it?

Being of an impatient and impetuous nature, it didn't take her long to decide. Of all the people she knew who seemed to know how to go it alone, cut themselves off from the past (particularly their elders' stuffy past), and follow their own Grail, it was surely the brave flappers.

She, Zena, famous for her bravery, would pull herself together and become a flapper.

She lit the lamp on her night table, hopped out of bed and went to the cheval looking glass. In front of this glass where one saw—and did not see—oneself, she tried on flapperdom. She turned her hair under to see how it would look bobbed; being so silky, it slipped and slithered, but she got the idea. Not bad, she said, really thinking it looked marvelous, rather more like a medieval page than a flapper, however. . . . She let her hair slip down and went into the flapper's slouch. Back and forth, she walked in front of the mirror, slouching, pouting, and smiling cynically. Slouching would take more practice (Mama had been very strict about posture) and would have to include the wearing of a bandeau to flatten her breasts. (She did wish flappers weren't *that* boyish.)

Just before she fell asleep, she practised the call of "Whoopee!" It had been the worst day in her life and it had exhausted her. It was a low keyed little whoopee that she called.

As luck would have it, it was the next day that Zena saw the flapper clutching her head. The flapper was sitting on the grass, leaning against a maple tree. Her face was only slightly less green than the tree's early leaves.

"Is something wrong?" Zena asked, running up to her.

"No, nothing," the flapper moaned. "Nothing at all except that I wish I was dead."

"Oh, no!" Zena cried.

"Oh, yes!" the flapper moaned some more and streaks of black mascara slid down her green cheeks as she began to cry. "I have been unlucky in love. I have been jilted. I have had too much to drink. Dead, dead, dead, I wish I was dead—"

"*You* have been jilted? Oh dear—if *you* can't be lucky in love then who can?" Zena cried.

"How should I know?" the flapper moaned.

A poet with long hair and flowing tie, who had walked all the way up from Greenwich Village, had stopped to stare at the flapper and to listen.

"By cocktail time tomorrow, this flibbertigibbet will have forgotten her death wish and today's unhappy love and be off to a new one. In the years ahead, we are all going to forget, we are all going to pretend that it was more fun than it was. The sound of whoopee rings empty over the land, there is another sound I hear, it is the sound of woe-unto-us—"

"Oh, do tell him to shut up," the flapper begged, "my head is splitting. A hangover is bad enough, a bad poet is worse."

"Ignoramus!" the poet shrieked.

"Spoilsport." the flapper moaned.

It was the last word she spoke before her eyes closed.

"Help! Help!" Zena yelled.

"Shh! Shh! You'll wake her up," the poet scolded. "She's sleeping like a baby."

Asleep, the flapper did look like a baby, a pale green one.

Zena took a long, thoughtful walk. Well . . . maybe not a flapper. . . . Painful as it was, she had to admit that she was discouraged and heartsick, that she herself was disillusioned and disappointed with Love. Maybe she should renounce Love altogether . . . maybe she should get herself to a nunnery . . . if that was too extreme . . . then what . . . ?

CHAPTER 13

I T DID SEEM as though the very heavens were in-
volved. Storms burst from them quite out of season,
damaging early plantings and irritating people who
liked their weather and their morning coffee on schedule.

"Oh, dear, the world is an untidy mess, isn't it?" Benedicta asked the world at large as she tried to cross a
gutter swirling with rainwater.

"Do stop talking to strangers," Cassandra scolded.

The streets were deserted. It being spring, the deser-
tion was all the more marked. The organ grinder with
his little monkey was not out. Nor the Hokey Pokey
man who sold ice cream. Nor the scissors grinder. Nor
the German trios who played in the alleys and the court
yards for the pennies that would be thrown out of windows. No one was out who didn't absolutely have to be.

Cassandra and Benedicta were out because Cassandra had to leave a calling card at the house of a lady recently become rich, and Benedicta was out because she had to leave calf's foot jelly at the house of a lady recently become poor.

"Dear," Benedicta gasped, "dear, that isn't—that couldn't be *our* Zena coming out of the *public* library, is it?"

"Where?"

"There."

"It is."

"But Cassandra—germs, all those germs, *strangers'* germs. We are not acquainted with the strangers who handle those books, read those books, are we?"

"Worse, we don't know *what* books Zena reads there."

"Shall we call out to her?"

"Certainly not. Kindly remember that we are ladies, not fishwives."

"Yes, dear. But—unless I am very much mistaken I believe our Zena is carrying something."

"What?"

"A book, dear."

"A *book?* From the *public* library? How strange, how very strange."

"And naughty, very naughty when she has so many nice clean books in her very own private library. I do wonder why, don't you?"

"I intend to find out."

* * *

Professor Schmidt smiled as he walked the rainy windswept streets. Every Tuesday afternoon at this time he smiled. A man is bound to smile as he takes such a long walk from a land of shadows into the sun, he told himself. On Tuesdays, it had become his habit to talk to himself in this style. On all other days of the week, when he walked he walked with Bach.

This Tuesday, he stopped for a long time in front of a florist's window filled with spring flowers—daffodils and irises and lilacs shimmering behind the rain streaked glass.

Professor Schmidt had never bought a flower in his life, not even for his dear mother. Before too long, he knew, the girl with the yellow hair would be a young lady who would receive many flowers. He saw the long slender white boxes, the green tissue paper, and the little white cards. He did not permit himself to see what would be written on those cards. He was not a man to read other people's mail. But ah, if he were only younger. But was he not old enough to be avuncular? On the spur of the moment he decided that, avuncular, he would be the first to bring a flower, one perfect flower. How much could one perfect flower cost, he wondered, thinking about his lunch the next day?

Two silk umbrellas skimmed through the slanting rain. Then bumped into each other.

"Zena—I have something to tell you."

"Yes, Vera? Is it about Bernice?"

"No. It's about me. Zena, I have a date."

"You have a date. That's nice."

"Zena—I said I had a *date*. Are you sick or something?"

"Something."

"You look funny."

"Thank you for the compliment."

"Don't you even want to know who I've got a date with?"

"Alban Kroop's twin brother."

"Silly. He doesn't even have a brother."

"That's something to be grateful for."

"Neither rain nor sleet nor dark of night shall stay these swift couriers from their appointed rounds," a voice boomed. "Girlies, make way, make way."

It was the United States mailman carrying his sack over his shoulder. The umbrellas made way, then came together again.

"Zena, it's a blind date."

"That's the best kind."

"Zena, you are funny, you are *very* funny. I think you're coming down with something."

"I'm coming down all right."

"Zena, guess where we're going to meet. Guess."

"There?"

"You guessed. When he said under the clock at the Biltmore, I thought I'd faint with excitement. Harvard, Yale, Princeton, Vassar, Wellesley, Smith. That's where they meet each other, under the clock at the Biltmore. It's the most famous place in the world for boys and girls to meet each other—" Vera stopped short.

121

"Zena! Why Zena, your eyes, they've turned blue. Oh, Zena!"

"It's the rain. The rain is making me sad. Vera, have a lovely date, a divine date, a perfectly divine date. And, and give my regards to all the boys and all the girls under the clock at the Biltmore."

Zena clutched the book tightly and walked on in the rain, her eyes becoming more and more blue.

Professor Schmidt waited nervously for the door to be opened.

To bring someone a flower was harder on his poor worn nerves than he would have imagined. Perhaps he ought to pretend that it came from an overflowing vase in his own home? But the power to imagine such an object in his barren little apartment failed him. Besides, he was clumsy at deception.

To quiet his nerves, he began to hum from the courante of Bach's Suite No. 1 in C Major; sometimes he thought if it were not for Bach his sanity would be threatened; no one and nothing quieted him like Bach.

A new maid opened the door. This one was unusually doleful, acting almost as if—as if this were a house of mourning?

"Who shall I say—?" she whispered.

"Professor Schmidt, the piano—" he whispered back. "Has anything—?"

But she was gone in a gloomy whispering of starched uniform.

Professor Schmidt waited for the patter of feet to

come racing toward him; usually she called out gaily and at the sound of her voice, he would begin to feel his perpetual chill leave him.

It was taking too long and a terrible sense of foreboding deepened his chill. Had indeed someone—? Professor Schmidt could never bring himself to call death by its name. But his ears which were sensitive to true pitch listened for a clue.

At last he heard a footfall, heavy and slow.

Professor Schmidt began at the beginning, the overture of the C Major.

"Professor Schmidt—"

He barely recognized the voice.

Zena's face was blue white, as if the cream had been skimmed from it. And something, or someone, had pulled the yellow hair back tight enough to pull it out by the roots.

"Professor Schmidt, I have something to tell you—"

Breathing hard through his catarrhal nose, he presented the flower wrapped in green tissue paper.

Zena took it without looking at it. "Thank you very much, Professor Schmidt." Silence. "Professor Schmidt, I will not be taking any more lessons."

Professor Schmidt fumbled his way to a chair, a narrow seated, high backed Jacobean one, one capable of propping him up. "It's only a foolish little flower, a souvenir of the season—"

"You see I have changed my—plans."

The Professor's head sank lower on his chest.

"Now it is my plan to be a nurse."

The Professor lifted his head with some difficulty. "A noble profession," he said weakly.

"Thank you," Zena said, dropping her eyes modestly.

The Professor managed to pick up his coat, but could not manage to say goodbye. Outside, not even Bach could console him.

Zena unwrapped the green tissue paper. Professor Schmidt did not know his seasons. A perfect yellow rose is not a spring flower.

CHAPTER 12

THE CHAIR was cold. The library was all cold brown leather—cold, slippery, and squeaky. Shakespeare in marble looked down at her, his little smile sweeping through the centuries, amused, undisturbed, and unsurprised, having predicted everything.

"You were wrong about one thing, Shakespeare." Zena addressed him: " 'For never was a story of more woe than this of Juliet and *no* Romeo . . .' "

"Self-pity makes for dewlaps." Crystal drifted in mournfully, like a fragile leaf drifting to its doom.

Zena studied a book, which was lying closed in her lap, one which had come from the public library, not this most private one.

"When your mama comes home from her travels and takes a look at you—"

Zena opened the book.

" 'The patient with a bed sore is a patient with an indolent nurse,' " she read. Her tone was severe, giving notice that she did not wish to be disturbed, that she wished above all else to be allowed to pursue her life's work without interruption.

"I warned you. You can't say I didn't warn you." Crystal pointed a warning finger at Zena. "You are now suffering from shock, pure and simple. It is not a vocation that will cure you, but sulphur and molasses."

Zena closed that book and opened a second one and studiously read: " 'The very first canon of nursing, the first and the last thing upon which a nurse's attention must be fixed, the first essential to a patient, without which all the rest you can do for him is as nothing, with which I had almost said you may leave all the rest alone, is this: *To keep the air he breathes as pure as the external air, without chilling him.*' " Zena thought about this. "What else does a person breathe except external air?"

"*You* ought to know. Hot air. That's what silly girls who don't listen to their elders breathe. As I was saying—"

" 'Effluvia from excreta,' " Zena continued to read, " '. . . of the fatal effects of the effluvia from the excreta it would seem unnecessary to speak.' "

"Does your Aunt Cassandra know you are reading this?"

Zena flipped the pages.

" 'Noise: The fidget of silk and crinoline . . .' "

"Crinoline?"

" 'Burning of the crinolines: Fortunate it is if her skirts do not catch fire—and if the nurse does not give herself up a sacrifice together with her patient, to be burnt in her own petticoats.' "

Crystal sat down.

"Ducky, nursing is not for you. It's too extreme. With you it's all or nothing . . . with such a temperament perhaps a career in the theatre . . . ?"

" 'Indecency of the crinolines: . . . A respectable elderly woman stooping forward, invested in crinoline, exposes quite as much of her own person to the patient lying in the room as any opera dancer does on the stage. But no one will ever tell her this unpleasant truth.' "

"And who may I ask wrote this unladylike book?"

"Miss Nightingale."

"Miss Nightingale? Miss *Florence* Nightingale? Our very own *English* Miss Nightingale?"

"Herself. None other. These are her notes on nursing."

"I declare! How extraordinarily un-English of her." Crystal was fiddling with her apron pocket and studying Zena with sad, worried eyes. "Why does your hair have to be skinned back that way, like a skinned rabbit's?"

Zena put the book down with a big sigh. "My dear Crystal, it so happens that nursing is not for flibberti-gibbets. It is for *serious* women, serious *looking* women." She paused. "It also happens that I *feel* like a skinned rabbit."

Crystal shook her head as if it was all too much for

her. "Sulphur and molasses," she murmured absent-mindedly, still fiddling with her apron pocket. "Ducky, you were going after love too hard, as if the goal was to win the championship at Wimbledon. Tennis is one matter; love, I'm sure, is another. Love is a most mysterious affair. So I am told. The more mysterious the better. So I understand."

Zena's eyes had turned the blue of a rain washed sky. "It is now my intention to love humanity, that's who."

Crystal shuddered. "Noble, fiercely noble. Personally, I favor love that is more personal."

"Each to his own. What have you in your apron pocket?"

"Oh? Oh, yes." Crystal made a weak attempt at pretending to have just had her memory jogged. Slowly and reluctantly she reached into the pocket. "This came in the afternoon post."

There is no mistaking an envelope that encloses an invitation to a wedding. This one was of a creaminess and a richness that virtually reeked of orange blossoms and played the wedding march.

"Of course you will decline. 'Miss Zena regrets—' " Crystal's voice was strained with worry.

Zena ripped open the outer envelope, then the inner one. A tiny square of tissue paper floated to the floor. ". . . requests the pleasure of your company . . ."

"Everyone loves a wedding." Zena spoke just above a whisper. "Remember how we used to stand outside a church whenever the canopy was up and the red carpet was out? Everyone loves a bride. Poor Bernice . . ."

"Zena, I am warning you. From the bottom of my heart I am warning you *not* to go to *this* wedding."

Zena was running her fingers over the raised engraving of the invitation.

"Because *he* will be there?" she asked.

"Yes, yes. I'm warning you—"

"Crystal—" Zena spoke quietly. "Crystal—instead of so much warning, why didn't you explain?"

"*Explain?*" Crystal's mouth remained open.

"Crystal, you may as well give up. I've guessed. He was my mama's matchmaker, wasn't he?"

Crystal sank back in her chair.

"Was he, or wasn't he?" Zena prodded.

"You're forcing me. I'm doing it against my will. I was sworn to secrecy. Your mama keeps her secrets more secret than anybody else. It's her pride, her hurting pride. In my whole life, I never saw such pride . . ."

"Do please stop rambling and start explaining."

"Ducky, it's not an easy story to believe. I won't blame you, if you don't believe a word of it."

"I'm ready to believe anything—now."

At least, I hope I am, Zena thought, and steeled herself to listen with cool detachment.

Crystal cleared her throat nervously. "A story long untold gets stuck in the throat, does not unwind like silk." She cleared her throat again. "Mind you, there's no proof. But it has always been my private opinion that it is a tale of unrequited love and revenge."

"Love? Revenge? One of those trite tales?"

129

"I don't have to go on, your royal highness . . ."
Zena waved her hand royally. "Pray do. I have a weakness for love stories as you well know . . ."

"You can say that again. Well, since she didn't love Jabez, he mismatched your mama to your papa out of revenge. That's my opinion."

"Revenge? Mismatch? My papa was no mismatch, he was handsome, very handsome. My papa was no ugly frog." Forgetting her cool detachment, Zena's voice was rising.

"Zena, how many times have I told you handsome is as handsome does? Your papa may have been handsome, but as husbands go, he went—away that is."

"You mean he *deserted* my poor mama?"

"Poor Mama. *And* poor Papa too. Fair is fair. He was never allowed to finish sentences in this house, that's what did it. A man can get all choked up with unfinished sentences. Come to think of it, so can a woman. Not that the poor man didn't have a natural weakness for horses. Where the horses ran, there ran he."

"A poetic tale too—"

"Sarcasm makes for—" Crystal broke off. "Where was I?"

"At the race track."

"Oh, yes. Well, your mama was most horribly angry at Jabez for mismatching her to a gentleman who ran after horses. She fired him as the family matchmaker."

"Three cheers for Mama."

"Ah, but he refused to stay fired." There was a note of fear in Crystal's voice. "To speak plainly, he is not an easy man to fire. You can see that, can't you, ducky? I mean he comes and goes as he pleases you might say, mightn't you?"

"I certainly would."

Then, Zena remembered the ash in her hand when the card had been burned.

"But—he seems to have fired himself." And she told Crystal about it.

"It's nothing but a trick to confuse you. Believe me. Confuse and conquer, that's his motto. Ducky—I haven't told you the worst of it—"

Zena sat up as straight as she could in the slippery chair.

"Ducky, there is a price on your head."

Zena's heart began to pound.

"From the day you were born. A price put on the head of a wee innocent baby. He took one look at you and said, '*That*,' pointing his finger directly at you so there was no mistaking whom he meant, '*that* is to be my crowning glory, my masterpiece, for *that* I will make the greatest match of my career.' I can see it all as if it was yesterday. The sun had been pouring into the south chamber. Suddenly, it went behind a cloud. All was darkness in that room. Your mama, who is famous for her bravery, spoke. She said you were to be no such thing, that when the time came she herself would be your matchmaker, none other. In that room there was a battle of wills that rattled the pictures on the walls. I am sorry to say your mama lost."

"What does that mean?"

131

"Blackmail. Blackmail of a most dastardly brand. If he was not to be your matchmaker, he threatened to tell the whole world that you were born out of wedlock."

Zena could feel her face tighten as the blood drained from it.

"*My* mama—?"

Crystal did not answer, but Mama's presence was before them, Mama so strong and strange—and made vulnerable by pride. Vulnerable, easy to wound; wounded by Papa, wounded by Jabez. Now to be wounded by gossip and laughter. Zena stifled a sob and once again struggled for cool detachment to ask the question that had to be asked.

"Well—was I? Am I?"

"Zena! Are you crazy? *Your* mama? Certainly not."

"Then what's all the fuss about? No one would believe him."

"Zena, it is a terrible fact of life on this earth that if there is anything your precious humanity is fond of believing, it is the worst. And your yellow hair doesn't help. On both sides of your family, as far back as anyone can go, there is only black hair, not a yellow thread among them. So you see it would be only too easy for humanity to believe that—well, that your papa was not your papa."

"But he was. I never saw him in my life but I know he was. My poor mama—"

"Yes. Her pride, her dignity. She has been a good mistress to me—"

And a good Mama to me, Zena thought, in her own

strange, special way.

They sat silently in the library, with Shakespeare smiling down on them.

"And all this because of unrequited love?" Zena asked, after a while.

"In my opinion."

"It's too much."

"It's more than that."

"I would like to ask a question."

Crystal sagged with exhaustion. "It certainly is your right," she said, weakly.

"How is it you people didn't protect me from him? With a duenna? Secret police?"

"Are *we* magicians? Are *they* magicians?"

Zena became very thoughtful, chewing on a strand of yellow hair.

"And neither am I a magician," Zena said. "Oh, now I wish you hadn't told me all this."

"Why is that?"

"Why? Think about it. I never did care to be a martyr."

"You would have found out sooner or later. Jabez would have seen to that." Crystal did a belated take. "*Martyr?* Don't you go getting any more of your fancy ideas into your head. We've had more than enough of those. If there's anything gets my back up, it's a martyr."

"But if he tells the whole world? And—and I have it in my power to stop him?"

"You'll do nothing of the sort. I won't let you. Your

mama won't let you." Crystal's energy was returning and she clapped her hands. "Libel! That's what we'll do, we'll threaten him with a libel suit. It's a wonder we never thought of that before."

"Libel? Crystal you're being silly. How are you going to get hold of him for a libel suit?"

Crystal collapsed again. "You have a point there."

"Oh, Crystal, what is to become of me?"

Crystal covered her face with her apron.

Zena picked up the invitation to the wedding, studied it, ran her finger over the engraving again.

"Crystal?"

There was no sound from behind the apron.

"Crystal, I—I have decided to go to this wedding after all."

Crystal uncovered her face.

"No!"

"Yes! I will plead with him—"

"*Him?* He has the devil's own deafness."

"To play safe, I will do something else too. I will save my mama by making myself so ugly that he will not want to be my matchmaker any more."

Crystal groaned.

CHAPTER 15

I T WAS A PLACE of blue and gold, of gilded candelabra and chandeliers, of many mirrors. It was a place famous for its great balls, its fabulous debutante parties, its grand weddings. It was a place famous for magic.

"Is this the hotel where all his weddings happen?" Zena asked Crystal.

"Every one of them, except those that take place in the palaces of Europe, of course. The receptions that is. The ceremonies take place in this or that church, sometimes in the palace itself, sometimes here—as it will tonight—whatever his whim dictates. It cannot be denied that when it comes to his weddings, he is a very fussy man. The introductions take place elsewhere. The Plaza perhaps, or an exclusive club—elsewhere. Never, *never* that Biltmore where boys and girls meet each

135

other without the assistance of Mr. Jabez. Now *there's* a clock that devil would like to tinker with, I'll wager. There's a clock that is the enemy of his profession. Incidentally—when you went sleigh riding with that strange boy, he stopped your mama's clock to warn her and to remind her that there were to be no strange boys in your life because *he* was to be your matchmaker come hell or high water." Crystal sighed gloomily. "But wherever the introduction, here, here is where it ends, the happy ending."

"And—and is this where my mama and my papa were married?"

"The very place. And what a wedding it was! Fit for royalty. Your mama's gown came from Paris. How royal she was that day. And your papa—what a handsome prince he was. But mind you, the way that Jabez looked at your mama and your papa that day gave me a chill. Unrequited love, I said to myself, if ever I saw it. And up to no good is that red-headed devil—I added to myself. Up to no good." Crystal lowered her voice and glanced around anxiously. "Did you just hear a footstep?"

Zena had not. Her attention was elsewhere. They were walking toward a reflection in a mirror. The woman with the ancient black straw sailor on her head was walking as a duenna should beside a girl whose yellow hair was pressed down to a skin tight skull cap and whose crepe de Chine dress, hanging limply, was more suitable for Saturday morning dancing class than a grand wedding at this grand hotel. They were strangers, those two figures in the mirror.

"What a touching sight we make," Crystal said, straightening her hat. "The duenna and the tragic young heroine. But I do wish we had settled on a more tragic frock for you. What amuses though, ducky, is that incognito though you are, they still turn to stare at you."

Zena smiled wanly. "Isn't it time to go in?"

"Morbid, aren't you?"

Zena nodded.

"But must you also drag your feet?"

Zena nodded again.

Yes, she must. Being tragic was exhausting wherever one was; here, it was more exhausting. Besides, it was absolutely necessary to drag her feet because suddenly, inside her, like a rowdy jack-in-the-box, there was another girl clamoring to get out; this girl was wearing a sea green chiffon dress, her yellow hair was in a soft chignon, her feet were twitching to dance, her arms were outstretched, she was calling out, laughingly, here you have been waiting for me and here I am, here I am—

"Quick, quick. Curtsy, curtsy," Crystal ordered.

Zena bent a stiff knee.

"Who was that?" she asked.

"Oh, some queen or other. They do so love to be recognized."

Zena barely turned her head: She was ordering that other girl to go right back where she came from.

At last Crystal brought them to the grand stairway

137

with its iron balustrade and its steps curved in sinuous flight.

The wedding guests ascending there were a mixed bag of dowagers and young matrons, of many elderly gentlemen and a sprinkling of young gentlemen. Miss De Koven's School for Young Ladies was represented. Among them were some reigning belles in clouds of chiffon.

Oh, Zena dear, how *sweet* you look, they called out kindly now, who, in that other time, that almost forgotten time, had been so unkind.

Vera, the maid of honor, marcelled and even powdered, a pink rose in layers of chiffon petals, was smiling and chatting on the arm of a young man.

"Oh, Zena dear, how *sweet* you look," Vera called out.

All this sweetness and light tasted of arsenic. But there was one comfort, ice cold comfort to be sure: The young men were sad as they glanced Zena's way.

Suddenly, without any warning whatsoever, Crystal grabbed Zena and tried to pull her back. It was, of course, too late.

Jabez stood there looking, if the truth must be told, magnificent in his white tie and tails. Everyone turned to gape at him; some appeared to recognize him; some did not.

However, he had eyes only for Zena, eyes that were disturbingly amused, as they traveled over the limp crepe de Chine dress, the hair pulled back.

When Zena saw this man she had once had such faith

in, had even loved, she wanted to stay; she wanted to run. Her eyes were black with fury, and her belly was knotted with fear. Her confusion was such that she almost forgot the main reason for being there.

Jabez spoke: "What a pity it is to see such self-destructive anger in one so young. My dear Crystal, had you no sage words of advice to keep this young lady from this ridiculous masquerade?"

"I begged her to run for her life, that was my advice."

"Dear, faithful Crystal, of course you did. But a country woman like you knows better. It was rather like telling the salmon swimming homeward to turn about and do a backstroke, wasn't it?"

Zena barely listened; she was intent on recalling herself to her mission.

"Jabez," she interrupted, "Jabez, Crystal told me the secret."

"Dear, faithful Crystal."

"Sir—I came to beg you to please, please not hurt my mama—*please*, sir—"

"So many pleases. Charming to see such filial devotion, is it not, Crystal?" Jabez lit a cigarette, but his hand actually did appear to tremble.

"Charming, charming." Crystal echoed automatically, watching Jabez as closely as if he were a snake about to spring.

"Since you have been told the secret, you are aware of the conditions that govern my not hurting—as you put it—your mama, are you not?"

"That's why I came here—to beg you to resign as my

matchmaker without slandering my mama. Please, sir."

"Please sir? I see. Just like that? Just because you wish it? Oh, the arrogance of the young. Don't you find it so, Crystal?"

Crystal tugged at Zena. "Come, Zena." But Zena was not ready to give up.

"Sir, sir, I confess that I'm mixed up. When you burnt the card, I thought you were finished with me, that you no longer wanted to be my matchmaker, but Crystal said . . ."

Crystal rushed in. "It was a trick, I told her it was a trick."

"Ah, leave it to a country woman to know a trick when she sees one. Nature's full of them, isn't she?" His face suddenly darkened. "Trick or no trick. I do not care to be called the False Enchanter, the Great Traitor, etcetera, etcetera. I do not care for this conversation either. Listen to me well. I am immune to pleas. And I am only moderately amused by your childish attempt to look ugly. When it comes to tricks, you need to learn a thing or two."

"I can see that, sir," Zena said, with despair. "Sir, could I please ask one or two questions?"

"No. This is a gala, a festive occasion. This is not the time for questions and answers."

Crystal grabbed hold of Zena. "Come, Zena, come before this devil—"

Jabez laughed. "She doesn't want to leave. She wants to see the wedding. Everyone loves a wedding. Even the wedding of a frog. Is not that so, dear child?"

"Why did you do that to poor Bernice? Why?"

"*Poor* Bernice? Really! The young are boring, are they not, dear Crystal? The child must learn that self-centeredness, self-indulgence, self-deception, and sentimentality makes for—what, dear Crystal? Near-sighted squinty eyes, perhaps?"

Crystal's mouth was shut tight, into a thin hard line.

"Ah, cat's got your tongue, which reminds me—" Jabez looked around the red carpet. "He does so hate these scenes. Well, to get back to the subject at hand. I will refresh your memory. The frog *did* turn into the prince. Did he not?"

"That was in a fairy tale."

"And what do you think you're in?" Jabez asked. "But all jokes to one side, for those who look there's more to fairy tales than meets the eye—" Jabez turned away and seemed to be looking for someone.

"Jabez, please—once more—what about my mama?"

Jabez pretended not to hear.

"Then . . . what about *me?*"

"When the time comes, you'll find out."

"What does that mean?"

"That is for me to know and you to find out." Jabez's smile was terrifyingly secretive. "In the meantime, do stay and enjoy the wedding. Besides, the artist who does my wedding receptions has been waiting to meet you since the day you were born. As Crystal told you, you were to be my crowning glory, for you I was to have made the greatest match of my career. Ah well, now here you are in this silly masquerade. He too will be amused."

"Come, come!" Crystal tugged at Zena.

141

But curiosity once killed a cat. Zena understood why. The habit of being curious was pernicious. She stood still.

Jabez nodded and a gentleman appeared. He was a sad faced gentleman, as elegant as Jabez in white tie and tails.

"The patron," Crystal whispered, "the most famous hotelkeeper in the world."

Jabez murmured to the patron. The patron began at the tip of Zena's shoe: Skillfully—with the skill of his profession—he took her measure without the slightest change of expression.

"*Oui*," he said, sadly, "you are right. I have seen *les reines*, *les princesses*, *les marquises*, *mais jamais*, *jamais*, never, never . . . *Mon vieux, vraiment elle est unique.*"

Jabez smiled smugly. "I told you so. Even in this ridiculous getup."

The patron took Crystal's measure. He was known all over the world for his fanatic attention to detail, for knowing his guest's idiosyncratic wishes before they had invented them.

He bowed to Crystal. "The duenna wishes to stay."

It was a statement, not a question.

Crystal drew herself up.

"As a duenna should," the patron added authoritatively.

Although she trembled, Crystal gave Jabez a triumphant look. Jabez's lip curled slightly, as if this were the triumph of a flea.

The patron beckoned to a *maître d'hôtel*. The *maître*

d'hôtel said *oui*, he would convey the order to the proper captain: a separate table for two, *vite!* All this in French, every word of it.

Zena turned to study Jabez's face.

He had disappeared.

"Where—?" Zena's voice rose.

The patron put his finger to his lips and waved toward the stairs.

Crystal pointed to the hat in her hand.

The patron frowned and threw up his hands.

"But of course!" He snapped his fingers and a maid came forward and took Crystal's hat.

"Tonight I am not quite myself," the patron said with a glance at Zena.

Crystal forgave him.

They managed the famous stairs quite well, everyone thought; the duenna and the tragic heroine.

The room was a bower of orange blossoms and smilax and white roses. The wedding guests were seated on slender gilt chairs, waiting. The bride's guests were separated from the groom's guests by a strip of red carpet which led to a lectern banked with more orange blossoms and roses.

Not waiting for an usher to seat them, Crystal and Zena found two seats in the last row next to the wall. Zena kept her eyes on her lap, where her fingers played here's the church, here's the steeple. But once or twice, when she couldn't resist raising her eyes for a morbid look at the lectern, she couldn't help noticing that the sparse sprinkling of young men were all uneasily, unhappily squirming on their chairs as they ogled her: Peculiarly, they acted as if *she* were betraying *them*. She didn't care, because they were a singularly unattractive lot. Naturally, considering that they were friends of the groom.

Behind potted palms fiddles tuned up. Too soon, the opening strains of the Wedding March. There was a rustle as dowagers and young matrons, anticipating moist eyes, reached for their handkerchiefs.

Zena intended to keep her own eyes dry as dust. In the last analysis, one always had one's will power. She now knew what they meant when they called comfort cold: She felt a chill on the nape of her neck.

The wedding guests turned to the rear of the room.

Zena would say one thing: The bridal gown was beautiful.

And the bride. Well, Zena knew the look on the bride's face, knew it well. The bride was pretending to have spotted some rare warbler.

And the groom? In white tie and tails, the frog looked like a frog that had been crossed with a penguin. It did not improve him.

Adieu, Bernice, adieu. Please forgive me, please. . . .

Zena kept her eyes on her lap until it was all over.

All the other tables had white roses and sprays of orange blossoms: the little table set up for Crystal and Zena had as its centerpiece one single yellow rose, perfect of course.

Zena made no secret of the fact that she began to itch all over.

Crystal said that upper-class young ladies itched in

private. However, she signaled the *maître d'hôtel*. He issued an order to the captain, who in turn issued an order to the waiter. The yellow rose was removed.

Behind more potted palms, they began to play a little Liszt, a little Chopin very softly. Involuntarily, Zena's eyes went across the room to Bernice at the bridal table. At the same moment, Bernice was turning toward Zena. She smiled broadly and waved to Zena.

Zena nodded back. Well, she did have to admit that among them, these artists had managed to transport Bernice here.

Thinking of artists, Zena said to Crystal: "Did you hear the patron say that he had seen queens and princesses etcetera, but he had never seen anyone like me, that I was unique?"

"I'm not deaf."

"Why am I unique?"

"Because the good Lord saw fit to spare the world the likes of more of you, I suppose."

"It was foolish of me to come here."

"Stubborn. Dangerous. And foolish. But now that we are here, let us enjoy the world's best kitchen—next to mine."

The menu was small, white, gilt-edged and exceedingly royal. *Truite saumonée royale* was among the glories of this glorious menu.

For once Zena had no appetite, not even for royal salmon trout.

This was noticed. She was presented with a bowl of fresh iced caviar. "Compliments of an unknown admirer," she was told in a discreet whisper. She couldn't

145

be discourteous: She devoured the bowl of caviar. This helped her to peck her way daintily through the rest of the dinner. She would say this much for the whole ghoulish event: The chef knew his business.

Ruffles and flourishes.

The Parade of the Wedding Cake.

She closed her eyes tight. She would rather die right there and then than see the frog cut Bernice's wedding cake.

When she opened her eyes, everyone was eating wedding cake, but her plate was empty.

Coming toward her in flying formation, were the patron, the *maître d'hôtel*, the captain, the waiter, and a busboy.

She was presented with a heart of strawberries on a bed of whipped cream.

"Mademoiselle, *compliments de la maison—Coeur des Fraises Zena.*

It became a famous specialty at that hotel.

She ate it, every last berry of it till there was no heart left: It was divine.

Then she felt sick to her stomach for the first time in her life.

This too was noticed. Before it was too late, in the nick of time, the waiter handed the *maître d'hôtel* a small bottle and a gold teaspoon.

"Mademoiselle, open your mouth."

She wasn't sure *that* was a good idea, but she did.

She swallowed the medicine: It was awful. But it worked.

Crystal breathed a sigh of relief. "The moral of this

tale, ducky, is don't eat your heart out."

"Very funny, very funny," Zena mumbled.

Behind the potted palms more ruffles and flourishes. The opening strains of a Chopin waltz.

The bride and the groom were to dance the first dance.

The wedding guests stood and applauded.

On the way to the dance floor, Bernice stopped at Zena's table. Leaning over Zena, from a cloud of wedding veil Bernice whispered, "Oh, Zena, I am so happy. I want to thank you from the bottom of my heart."

"You're welcome," Zena said, choking. "And I do hope you live happily ever after," she added, remembering her manners.

The bride picked up her train, the groom put his arm around her and away they went, round and round. Zena noticed that if one used one's imagination, one had the illusion that they looked the way a bride and a groom should.

Next, it was the wedding guests' turn to dance.

"I would like to go home now," Zena said.

Vera twirled past, still chattering as she danced. She fluttered some fingers at Zena.

No detail had been overlooked. A stag line waited on the edge of the dance floor to cut in on a dancing belle. These young men had it in their power to make or break a belle. "How many times were *you* cut in on tonight?" The girl with the highest score would be the reigning belle of belles.

The belles fluttered fingers at Zena.

"I insist upon going home now."

"You do not wish to catch the bouquet?"

Zena gave Crystal a scornful side glance.

"I am not tall enough."

"Ah, ducky . . ."

With the sound of the wedding celebration behind them, Zena and Crystal slipped out, their footsteps muffled by the thick carpets.

In the anteroom, where the cloakrooms were, it was quiet. No one was there but the matron who guarded the coats.

Zena took her coat, but lingered.

"Come, come," Crystal tugged at Zena's coat. "It is time to go and I for one will be happy to leave. It makes me nervous the way he sneaks in and out of this place."

Zena still lingered. In the mystery with which Jabez had seen fit to shroud the future, one question nagged to be answered: What if she wanted to—or had to—change her mind and accept Jabez as her matchmaker to save her mama, how would she tell him this without a card? Why—should this be the case—had he not given her one?

Just then, a young page, slim and trim in his uniform, came toward her. On the palm of his white-gloved hand he carried a small silver salver.

So, she thought, I am going to get a card after all.

"*Avec les compliments*—" the page presented the salver to Zena.

The silver was a perfect foil for one perfect yellow rose. Silver is also effective for keeping objects ice cold.

Zena stared at it. "No card? Isn't there a card?"

The page shrugged. "*Je regrette, mademoiselle,* no card."

He presented the tray with the rose again.

"No. Thank you, no. *Pour vous*—for you, a rose," Zena said, and walked away from the page. The page who had been trained to keep all his emotions strictly to himself while on duty, forgot himself and opened his mouth in utter amazement.

In this mystery, one thing was certain: A Jabez that one could not conjure up was more frightening than ever.

THERE BEGAN A TIME of shadows blotting out sunlight, of moonlight peopled with unnerving manifestations—strange glows and noises.

Why had there been no card? What mean evil trick did that magician have up his sleeve this time? Not that she *wanted* a card, heaven forbid, but what if she *needed* one? What if it became a matter of life or death? Mama without her pride, her dignity, would be more dead than alive, wouldn't she?

She had hoped that with Miss Nightingale's assistance she could eventually ignore questions about love. But had Miss Nightingale been right after all? (Questions inclined to breed like rabbits: Why?) Miss Nightingale had had some sharp words for ladies who turned to nursing after a disappointment in love, also for novelists who could find no better solution for their broken

150

hearted heroines. Indeed! said Miss Nightingale indignantly, it took more than a broken heart to make a nurse out of a nurse—or words to that effect.

The shameful truth was that Zena was not as eager to love humanity as she ought to be for such a noble profession.

One day, when the library had become much too much like a sick room, Zena decided she needed fresh air badly and went out for a walk.

Various people from various countries still claimed Zena as their own, but all were shocked at the change in her. The Italians thought that Venice, the city of lovers, would put the roses back in her cheeks. The French stuck by Paris in the springtime as the cure-all beyond compare. The Greeks knew that a journey to Delphi where the goddess would whisper words of wisdom was the answer. And the Austrians reluctantly wondered if this wasn't after all a case for their compatriot in Vienna, Sigmund Freud with his couch and his personal questions. However they differed in their cures, they were nations united in their sadness: There was much that was wrong, they agreed.

Oblivious, Zena walked beneath the sycamores and the oaks and the maples now in full leaf on Central Park West. The park itself she had declared out of bounds. As she walked, she saw that the awnings were beginning to sprout from the brownstones and from the apartment houses too. Soon, when Mama came home from her latest travels, they would migrate to the huge old house where the many verandahs were swept clean and cool by the breeze that came off the sea. There, she would lie on the swing on one of those verandahs and no doubt spend the summer pining away for want of something to love. She was impatient to get there, get anywhere that was out of sight of the castle.

Transported as she was to that Victorian verandah, she had not been watching where she was going, nor what was going on around her, so she could easily have missed it. But she didn't.

Sliding up the avenue, on the park side, the side she was on, she saw the black electric.

Now, logically speaking, Zena should have been pleased at this chance to get a card—should she need one. Instead, she was frantic to escape. But shut off on one side by the park's wall of solid, impenetrable stone, and on the other side by a stream of steadily flowing traffic, there was no escape.

So be it. She decided she would tell Jabez that his tricks didn't frighten her one bit, so he might just as well stop the nonsense and give her a card.

Armed with this intention, she stood at the curb and waited for the electric to stop.

It did not stop. It sailed right past her without so much as a nod from Jabez.

Zena walked to the nearest bench and sat down.

What was the meaning of this?

"I do not like it, I do not like it one bit," Crystal said, when she heard about it.

"Maybe I am free at last," Zena said gloomily, not believing it for one second.

"When love apples grow on a hedge of thorns, that's when you'll be free of him," Crystal said, twisting the strings on her apron.

They were sitting in Crystal's room. Crystal's room was across many borders; foreign. There was the brass bed, behind it the bundle of wolfsbane to keep away witches. There was the shabby trunk, strapped, locked, and never, never to be touched by anyone under any circumstances. There were the photographs of Parnell and Victoria, cheek by jowl. There was the photograph of the moustachioed man, sometimes called Shaun, sometimes John. When Zena was very little he was a cousin; later he became a friend.

"*Now* who is he?" Zena asked.

"Alas, now you are old enough to know he is a drowned lover."

"Oh, Crystal darling—"

"Pray don't Crystal me. It was a long time ago." Crystal picked up her crocheting, a seemingly endless bolt of Irish lace.

"Crystal, I'm fed up with nursing."

Crystal jabbed her crochet needle into the lace.

"Good. And I'm fed up with being a character. One can overdo these things. And to speak plainly, I'm also fed up with being Irish."

"You still have the English. I don't have anything."

"Self-pity makes for being tiresome."

"But what *am* I to do?"

"Zena?"

"Yes, Crystal?" Zena asked, eagerly.

"Zena—what if you were to try being normal just for once? You know, nice and lukewarm like everyone else. Normal isn't too bad. Come, ducky, give it a whirl, why don't you?"

"Lukewarm? With a scandal probably about to ruin my mama?"

"Ducky, I have a thought."

"I could use a good one . . ."

"*You're* fed up with nursing. I'm fed up with being Irish. Jabez could very well be fed up with you and your goings on. That being the case, he naturally does not wish to give you another card and—drives right past you. Did you ever think of that?"

Zena shook her head. "I don't believe it. I just don't."

"Hoity-toity. Vanity makes for curvature of the spine."

But Crystal fiddled nervously with the crochet needle, jabbing it in and out of the lace.

"I *know* he's up to something awful."

"Love—lovey—I will not lie to you. I know it too. He is bound to get even with your mama somehow, someplace, sometime. It is the nature of the devil."

When Mama returned from her travels, Zena did not wait to be kissed; she embraced and kissed her astonished mama lavishly.

"What is this all about?" Mama asked, as she handed Crystal her little black straw toque. "What happened in my absence?"

Neither Crystal nor Zena answered.

154

Mama clipped her pince-nez on her nose and examined first Crystal and then Zena.

"You have been talking too much," she said to Crystal.

"Yes, madam."

"*Why?*"

"I wanted to stop Miss Zena from going to the wedding. She went, madam. The red carpet was out for her. All the signs were there, madam. They are expecting Miss Zena. Soon, madam."

Mama went white. With anger? With despair? With unaccustomed fear? With Mama, one did not know.

"Zena, why did you go there? Why?"

"Because I was invited, Mama."

"Zena, come here."

"Yes, Mama."

Mama cupped Zena's chin. "You look dreadful. I won't have it. I forbid you to look dreadful. I forbid you to do anything—anything silly."

"But Mama—" Zena held up a strand of yellow hair.

Mama avoided looking at the yellow hair.

"Nonsense!" she said, her black eyes flashing. "Stuff and nonsense! I will take care of my own affairs myself, thank you very much."

"But Mama, they aren't just *your* affairs. There is me too. Your scandal is my scandal. Not that I care of course. Besides—Jabez is up to something. Crystal and I know he is."

Mama did not argue that point, and Crystal and Zena filled her in with the alarming details.

"Nonsense!" she said, when they were finished. "He is just counting on confusing and frightening you. I forbid you to allow him to succeed."

"Yes, madam."

"Yes, Mama."

It was then that the grandfather clock struck. Although it was four o'clock in the afternoon, the clock struck only once. But once was quite enough.

They all jumped, including Mama.

"Call the clockmaker," Mama said, stamping her foot. "I won't have it. I simply won't have it."

"Yes, madam."

"Yes, Mama."

"Stop yessing me," Mama shouted, stamping her foot again.

Franklin, the fat chauffeur, tiptoed past them carrying Mama's bags, muttering, "No, madam, no, madam . . ."

That night the Tribunal of Mamas went into session again.

"But Augusta dear," Zena heard Benedicta say, "I do understand, if I may be allowed to say so, that poor dear Bernice is *so* happy, that one might even be disposed to call it a marriage made in heaven? Perhaps, after all he would be good enough to do the same for Zena?"

Mama must have glared ferociously, because Bendicta added lamely, "It was only an innocent question. I meant no harm."

There was a ladylike clap of hands and Cassandra spoke: "Whatever have I been thinking of! The solution is an old one, tried and true, and so correct. The grand tour! Augusta, Zena is of an age now when to have made the grand tour before her debut could lend it brilliance. Br-r-r-illiance! Aha! Away she is whisked on the grand tour—Munich, Paris, Rome, Florence, Venice, ah-h-h-h."

Mama spoke: "My dear Cassandra and my dear Benedicta, why I bother to discuss my personal affairs with you two can only be the result of one undeveloped soft spot in my brain. Grand tour indeed! Must I remind you that the tour called grand is precisely the one Jabez regards as nothing more than his daily constitutional, a mere turn around the block? Need I remind you that short of a trip to the moon, *there is no escaping Jabez?* Geographically speaking, that is."

"And if one does not speak geographically, is there another means of escape?"

"Yes."

"Yes?" asked Cassandra and Benedicta together. "And what would that be?"

"Slander."

"Slander?" shrieked Cassandra and Benedicta.

"I shall allow myself to be slandered."

Zena heard two thumps in quick succession which could only mean that Cassandra and Benedicta had fainted ensemble.

And Mama?

Mama, the least likely person to do so, was standing fast for martyrdom. Mama, it turned out, must love her yellow-haired daughter more than anyone suspected, most of all her daughter.

Zena was overcome by a great wave of love for Mama.

"No," she said, "no, Mama, I forbid you to be a martyr for my sake."

Zena tiptoed away—unsteadily, due to knees suddenly become weak.

CHAPTER 17

A S IF THE whole wretched business could be dis-
solved in a pool of silence, they did not talk about
it to each other.

Mama's back, impossible as that may seem, grew
stiffer, Crystal became more English, going so far as to
restrict their desserts to trifles, fools, and syllabubs. And
Zena's eyes were nearly always blue, the blue of a seaside sky at summer's end, when the beach and the sky
belong only to the gulls and the pipers.

The summer on the verandah was not spent, as Zena
had planned, with pining away for something to love.
After all, there was Mama.

And there was the listening to laughter. Never did
Zena remember so much laughter. The breeze off the
sea blew it her way from verandahs near and far, from
the Stutz Bearcats racing back and forth, from the
dunes, the tennis courts, the country club. It was the

laughter of boys and girls, and flappers and lounge liz-
ards, and college men and college girls, and debutantes
and their stag lines. It was the laughter of saxophones
announcing the jazz age, the age of flaming youth. It
was a great summer for laughter.

For everyone but Zena.

One August night with heat lightning turning the
night world on and off, unable to sleep with all that
laughter, Zena stood at the window watching the lights
of a ship as it sailed eastward toward Land's End.
When the ship disappeared, a new light appeared on the
beach road. An eerie light, unearthly pale, moving
slowly, coming closer. Before she saw its ghostly
shadow, she knew what it was.

She had no intention of allowing herself to be frightened by a black electric, but a black electric sliding
effortlessly over a badly rutted sandy beach road in the
middle of a night torn by lightning was enough to ice
anyone's blood.

Did Jabez imagine that she was going to race
through the night in her nightgown to catch up with
him and beg him to take her back?

Well—?

Well, she would not. On the contrary, she would race
back to bed and pull the sheet up to block out laughter
and heat lightning and the headlight of an electric.

Although the rage for suntanning had not yet ar-
rived, Zena's skin turned a golden apricot as she walked
the beach and the dunes, and her yellow hair was
bleached almost white, which most pleased the Dutch
and the Danes. On the days when she forgot to be sad,

the apricot skin, the green eyes, and the sun bleached hair, sometimes blown loose, pleased everyone. Except the young men, in particular the stags from the stag line, who were more perplexed than pleased: Why did this green-eyed girl go to such lengths to avoid their glances? Were they not, these footloose, carefree, unattached young stags, the most sought after young men, the ones without whom no belle could be a belle?

Yes, yes, but they were also strangers; besides, with martyrdom hanging over her head, she was not free.

Once, on a distant dune, she thought she saw silhouetted against a sea gray sky a boy with the crest of a kingfisher. She had been tempted to wave to him, but what if it were the wrong young man? Or what if it was her loneliness playing tricks with her imagination? What if there was no boy with the crest of a kingfisher? What then?

But if there were such a young man, he might be interested in knowing that she no longer tried to knight anyone. But she would not tell him why—that it was because she did not want to know if she had lost the power to do so.

It was on the day that they returned to the many-gabled house in the city that the first unmistakable warning came.

Naturally, the most infamous gossip sheet of the day was not given house room in Mama's house, but gossip, as everyone well knows, spreads like wildfire.

It was in Mr. Obermeyer's Market on Columbus Avenue that Crystal heard it. Crystal was smelling a cantaloupe for ripeness when a German cook who was

Crystal's enemy read it to a gossip-greedy circle of cooks and butlers. The cook read with a voice loud enough to crack the baskets of eggs. "It reads here, 'Coming soon. An in-ter-esting i-tem about a cer-tain black-haired lady mag-nate and her yellow-haired daughter.' So? Very in-ter-esting, no?"

There was a very interested, very excited, titter from the circle as they all pivoted toward Crystal.

Crystal handed the cantaloupe to Mr. Obermeyer.

"And, Mr. Obermeyer, I will have *two* pounds of your very best fresh caviar, if you please," Crystal ordered loud and clear with her English accent flying the Union Jack.

"*Two* pounds? A celebration, Miss Crystal?" Mr. Obermeyer asked as his pencil flew over his pad.

"Rah-ther! Madam is celebrating with a bit of caviar and iced champagne. So festive, don't you quite agree?"

In spite of themselves, the circle broke to make a path for Crystal.

When Crystal came in, closing the door behind her, Zena was stretched out on her bed, the ear piece of the telephone held away from her ear as Vera went on and on about her summer romance.

"Divine . . . divine . . . divine . . ." Zena murmured on cue.

Zena took one look at Crystal's face and begged Vera to excuse her.

As Zena listened to Crystal, her eyes went from blue to the black of anger.

"Traitor! Blackmailer! Devil!" Zena shouted.

"Amen. Amen. But what are we to do?"

"I will dye my hair black, that's what."

Crystal opened her eyes wide. "The overlooked obvious. Why didn't we ever think of that before, when you were a wee babe?" She shook her head. "It won't do, Zena. It's too late in the game for that." Crystal collapsed into a little velvet slipper chair. "Oh, Lord, your poor mama, it will be hard on her."

"Yes. My poor mama—"

"Ducky, what are you going to do?"

Zena chewed on a strand of yellow hair.

"I think, I think I will take a walk."

Crystal pulled herself out of the chair. "That's a good girl. But mind where you walk. It's—it's dangerous out there."

"Where isn't it?" Zena asked.

"My, but you're growing up! At the door, Crystal paused: "Wait until your mama sees the bill for that caviar."

Caviar reminded Zena of the wedding. The wedding reminded her that for some perverse reason she had saved the royal menu. Now, for some reason, mysterious to her, she slipped the white and gold menu into the pocket of her dress.

Just as she left the room, the little French clock chimed frantically; without doubt, it was warning her, imploring her to stay safe in her room, her room, which was a girlish bower.

CHAPTER 18

THE FLAG FLYING over the castle was at half mast.

Why?

No one had died that she knew of, no President, no Governor, no Mayor. But then, civics was not one of her best subjects so she did not read the newspapers religiously.

The first whiff of autumn was blowing through the park and she wished she had worn a coat. One of Bernice's birds, a small speckled one, took off from an elm and headed south.

Zena began to pace back and forth on the court, as if it were a widow's walk. The role of beggar did not suit her; neither did that of martyr.

It was a cloudy day and, as she paced, without the sun to go by she lost track of time.

Her eyes were getting blacker and blacker, until the thought struck her that the flag was at half mast for *Jabez!*

The conviction grew, but curiously along with it there was no triumph, nor the great relief one would have expected. That, she imagined, would come later. After all, she had to admit that he had been a worthy opponent. With just a smudge of blue beginning to shade the receding black in her eyes, she took the menu out of her pocket and proceeded to tear it into little pieces.

"Not quite yet," the voice said. "I am alive and well and living—elsewhere."

Zena didn't jump; she leaned sideways, as if she had been hit, and watched as a scrap of menu blew away.

"And pray, do not litter. I detest litter."

Zena turned on him, her eyes black as night now.

"You—you—you—"

"Pray do not finish that sentence. I detest unladylike language in ladies. So you thought I was dead, did you? That would have been convenient for you, wouldn't it?"

"Yes, it would have been."

"I admire frankness."

"Jabez—? Sir—? Jabez—please—please, Jabez, can't you please be nice and bury the hatchet?"

"In a word, no."

"My mama will die—"

"You can save her. Only you."

"Oh!" Zena stooped and picked up scraps of menu.

"Thank you," he said, "for not littering."

"You're welcome. What *was* the game you were playing? Could I please know that?"

"A version of hide and seek. It is an ancient game. The less available, the more desirable a thing becomes."

"Oh."

"You came here to tell me that at last you are quite ready to be my client, did you not?"

If the sun had gone into total eclipse, it could not have gotten darker.

Zena lowered her head slowly, as if already she could feel the weight of disaster.

"Is that supposed to be a nod?"

Zena nodded.

"Good. An enlightened decision. We are both getting too old for children's games. So!"

As Jabez took out his little leather book and riffled through it, Zena concentrated on not weeping.

"Jabez?"

"Yes?" He kept on riffling.

"Jabez, I have forgotten how to play a little Liszt, a little Chopin."

"Practise."

"Jabez, supposing I don't crown your career? Supposing no one will want me now that I am so ugly?" She pulled her mouth down, making herself as ugly as possible.

Jabez laughed. "You forget that one man's meat is another man's poison. And vice versa."

He continued to turn the pages, frowning as he did so.

"Are you—are you looking for—? Do you have a certain person in mind?" She hated herself for it, but her voice quavered.

"Ah—" he said, "here we are. Just the thing."

Her heart stopped beating.

"Who is he?" she whispered.

"Oh, do pull yourself together. You have forgotten that Jabez is an artist. I have been waiting for this for a long time, ever since the day you were born. I will not rush it. I will enjoy it—even if you do not. First, there will be the tea dances, the dinner dances, possibly a great ball, a masque. At least you like dances and balls, don't you?"

"Once upon a time I had intended to."

"We will begin at a small dinner dance in a castle. How's that?"

Bewildered, she looked up at the castle towering over them.

"No, no," he said. "Don't be silly."

"But we have no castles here in America."

"Who said anything about America?"

"Oh, no!" she raised her voice in alarm. "Oh, no! I'm not going to strange countries with you. I won't! I won't!"

He spoke slowly and with precision. "You will go where I take you. Or—else—"

"I'll go. I'll go."

"No more interruptions. There is a castle and that is where we are going. The Saturday night of the Thanksgiving weekend. A—A gala."

"And—and where is this castle?"

Jabez pointed his gold pencil due north.

"North?" Zena asked.

"It is not a castle in Spain. North."

North was where the castles of tragedy were. Zena felt the cold in her bones.

She started to take her leave, when he said, "By the way, it will do you no good to make yourself as ugly as possible. Indeed it will only make matters worse."

She walked on. She would say this much for tragedy: It was good for your posture.

THE PRESIDENT, famous for being a man of few words, had made the Proclamation, and the people had responded with traditional turkey and trimmings. That year, despite the President's dour face, Thanksgiving was celebrated with high spirits: The cry of "Whoopee!" rang from coast to coast.

But on Saturday, Zena, kneeling on her window seat, saw the park deserted and desolate. The lake was dark and the starlings had ceased their chattering and were silently heading for home.

Zena counted the lights as they began to appear on the far side of the park.

"Rich man, poor man, beggar man, thief—thief—thief—doctor, lawyer, Indian Chief—Chief—Chief—Rich man, poor man, beggar man, Kroop—Kroop—Kroop—"

"Tonight the national dish is cold turkey," Crystal said, as she set a plate of it on Zena's dressing table.

"It's a *dinner* dance. Besides, I'm not hungry."

"You will need your strength."

Mama came in, a black lace shawl around black silk shoulders, black shadows under black eyes.

"I forbid you to go," Mama whispered, her voice trembling.

"What if I were to tell you I *want* to go?"

"I would say you were lying."

"What if I were to remind you that Bernice was given some choice?"

"I would tell you that that will not be so for you. Remember you are to be his *crowning* glory. Such crowns are usually singular."

"What if—" Zena faltered.

"What if I were to weep? Would that stop you?" And in the black pools of Mama's eyes there was a terrible stirring that almost did stop Zena. Almost.

"No, Mama, no, you are brave. Remember?"

"I will tie a string around my finger to remind myself." Mama kissed Zena and held her for a long minute, then she left with Crystal, the black silk and the starched uniform rustling in mournful counterpoint.

Zena began to undress in front of the cheval glass. Moving close to it, she noted that her eyes were the blue of forget-me-nots, not a speck of green in them. Green, green was the color of her eyes. Gone, gone, her Own True Love. Gone, gone forever.

Out there a doorman whistled for a taxi and a girl yodeled: "Whoopee!"

When it was time, Crystal came in. Her head was bandaged with a black scarf. As if that weren't dramatic enough, her arms were foaming and billowing with sea green chiffon.

"My shroud?" Zena asked.

"Now, now, let's not overdo it."

"Look who's talking. You with your black bandage."

Crystal picked up the silver hair brush. Her hand shook.

"I do wish everyone would stop shivering and shaking. It's making me seasick," Zena complained.

"Sit down, milady. First the hair and then the dress, methinks, milady."

"Oh, please don't. Once upon a time—"

"—there was a young princess—" Crystal crooned softly and began to brush the yellow hair.

"About your hair," Crystal said, her arm moving in large smooth circles as she brushed, "We shall ignore fashion. Nothing, ducky, is more upper class than that. A lovely soft chignon at the nape of your neck it shall be."

Crystal pinned Zena's hair up to the tune of *God Save the King*. When the last pin was in place, she stood back. "It rather suits you," she said severely. "I believe one might go so far as to say it tends to make you—not *too* bad looking."

She offered Zena a silver hand mirror: The strange young lady reflected there was inclined to agree.

"It used to be that when a young girl put her hair up for the first time, it was an occasion. Now with all this new-fangled bobbed hair—"

Zena was twisting her head this way and that.

"So this is called being grown-up," she said.

"Not quite, ducky, not quite."

"Now the dress?"

"Now the dress."

Zena stepped into the sea of chiffon; soft . . . soft. . . .

When the last tiny button had been buttoned, Crystal stood back again.

There was only the girl and the chiffon, tiers of it. No sequins, no bugles, no baguettes, no embroidery. The dressmaker had known what she was about; she had known that nothing more was needed than the girl herself.

Zena pivoted slowly in front of the cheval glass.

"*Now* am I grown-up?"

"Not quite, lovey, not quite."

Crystal hastily brushed her eyes with the hem of her apron.

Far away, at the front of the house, a bell rang and Zena's eyes went flame blue.

Crystal stopped weeping and picked up a black velvet cape with a little white ermine collar, white kid gloves, and a small bag made of seed pearls.

"Leave me alone," Zena whispered. "I'll be out in a minute."

Alone, Zena walked around her room. She passed her fingers over the souvenirs of her childhood—a battered Raggedy Anne doll, veteran of too much love and too

172

much anger, an Easter egg in which a shepherd and a shepherdess smiled eternally at each other, a silken fairy wand that had worked wonders one May Day of dancing round the May pole. When she touched the little French clock, it tinkled plaintively.

"Sh-h-h," she hushed it.

She took one last look around her room. As she walked toward the door, she paused to honor all people traveling through enemy lands, exiles, and small animals scurrying through midnight forests.

Jabez was waiting in the foyer, dressed in the full regalia of his calling—white tie, tails, and black opera cape. His face was a white mask; the eyes that flicked over Zena were secretive.

In that entrance and exit hall, not a word was spoken. Only the clocks tolled the passing minutes.

Silently, Crystal put the cape over Zena's shoulders, handed her the bag and the gloves. She kissed Zena on the forehead, gave Jabez the full blaze of her cold fury, and walked off humming, "Rule Britannia."

Outside, the night was cool on Zena's face. A boy and a girl walked arm in arm; the girl was wearing a chrysanthemum. Close by a group of young ladies and young men were tumbling over each other getting into a limousine. The joke was very funny; they couldn't stop laughing.

Zena pulled her cape close as Jabez led her toward the electric, almost invisible in the darkness. Inside, she sank into the soft back seat, felt herself enclosed in a casket of dove gray. Jabez pressed a button and the interior was bathed in pale gold. The light was dim, but still a drop of dew could be seen clinging to the yellow rose.

Jabez lowered the bar; the motor purred; the electric slid away from the curb.

Zena closed her eyes.

Everyone turned to stare at the black electric gliding soundlessly through the night, its passengers illuminated by the soft light. The red-haired man in the opera hat wore a strange smile, wore it like a boutonniere. And that girl! That yellow-haired girl riding with her head held high and her eyes shut tight!

Zena opened her eyes just as they were gliding past a Franklin limousine and a Minerva town car. In the Minerva, an old gentleman stared at Zena and blew her a kiss; the elderly lady at his side shook her finger playfully at him.

"We are going downtown. We are going south," Zena said.

"It is a pleasure to be with a girl who knows north from south."

"Why aren't we going uptown?"

"It is not my custom to go uptown."

"But you said—"

"I am always being misquoted. That's how you know you are famous, when they start to misquote you."

"But you said the way to the castle was *north!*"

Jabez shrugged. "So I have changed castles."

"Jabez, *where* are you taking me?"

"Sit back. Relax. Trust me."

"Trust *you?* Are you crazy?"

"There will be those who will say that I am. No matter."

"And what does that mean?"

"Ah! Patience. You will find out. In due course. Never rush an artist at work."

"Why is the light on?"

"One does not become famous by hiding in the dark."

"Stop this car. I want to get out."

"Keep calm. Look out the window like a good girl. I find the skyline very much to my taste. Beautiful, don't you agree?"

Zena touched the handle of the car.

"It's locked," Jabez said. "I told you to trust me, didn't I?"

"Jabez—I'm scared."

"You? Scared? How charming of you. I must tell you a secret. The brazen ones grate on my nerves."

"I will disgrace you. Your name will be mud from coast to coast."

Jabez sighed. "My name? It will be interesting to see. Please! Do stop making a fuss. My nerves. For a mysterious reason, I am not quite myself tonight."

"What mysterious reason?"

Jabez laughed. "Wouldn't you like to know! Naturally you would. I assure you—all in good time. In the meantime, take the advice of one who knows whereof he speaks—enjoy the mystery while it lasts. Ah, see? We are now approaching the Hotel Plaza, the scene of many of my most successful—ah, arrangements. An agree-

175

able hotel, the Hotel Plaza."

"Is that where?"

"No. We are not going there. Tonight, our destination is elsewhere."

A horse pulling a hansom neighed mournfully.

A pride of young men coming down the steps of the hotel took off their hats and waved farewell as the electric passed them by.

Jabez circled the fountain and headed down Fifth Avenue. They went past the St. Regis Hotel, past the Hotel Gotham; ahead of them loomed the traffic tower on Forty Second Street; down, down, they were going—

"Where are you taking me?" Zena's voice was getting smaller and smaller.

The silence was ominous.

Abruptly, the electric turned east. East was where Grand Central Railroad Station would be.

"I am being abducted," Zena said. "You won't get away with it."

At Madison Avenue they almost collided with a taxi traveling south. It was Jabez's fault. He was now driving badly, recklessly, as if possibly he too were getting frightened.

They turned south. Jabez slowed down. Slowly, slowly, they slid past the famous hotel with its colonnaded facade. A horn honked behind them, but Jabez would not be pushed. They rounded the corner of the famous hotel, heading west this time, and came to a halt.

Zena's throat tightened; she remembered this entrance, remembered it only too well.

The doorman came toward them.

"*Bon soir*, Mademoiselle Zena," the doorman said with an Irish accent as he opened the door.

It hadn't been locked at all.

The doorman helped her out, took a firm grip on her elbow, and guided her through the door of the hotel. Jabez was close at their heels.

Zena was taking her steps with great care, warily, as if one false move and she would be completely submerged. Everything seemed underwater, scented water, and it was only natural that the grand stairway should shimmer in and out of focus. Unnatural was the aspect of the figure guarding the stairway.

This figure came toward her and she saw that of course it was the patron. But his face had been altered; the sadness was unmistakably nursing an unaccustomed smile.

Zena froze: *Good God! They're marrying me off tonight!*

She tried to run, but was blocked by Jabez.

"Wait, wait—" Jabez said.

"*Attendez, attendez*," the patron echoed.

Jabez frowned at the patron. "Please. This is my scene. Yours comes later."

The patron accepted the correction. "*Oui*. After you."

Zena made another attempt to escape; she and Jabez sidestepped back and forth in front of each other.

"Stop!" Jabez ordered. "This is not the place for slapstick. Nor is it the night for it. This night is for high comedy. *N'est-ce pas?*"

The patron agreed.

"You have heard the voice of experience," Jabez informed Zena. "Now you must listen. When you have listened well, then if it is still your heart's desire, you may run. She may run. May she not?"

The patron and Jabez smiled at each other, each with his own peculiar smile, bowed to each other, shrugged.

In spite of her great apprehension, Zena had to admit that these two were beginning to engage her interest.

"I am waiting," she said, "for the snapper."

"The snapper?" the patron inquired. "What is it the snapper?"

As far as the patron knew, the snapper was a fish. Mademoiselle is waiting for a fish? *Pourquoi?* Why? The patron who was famous for his attention to the most whimsical of whims did not wish to be caught slipping.

Jabez assured him that it was he, Jabez, who would provide the snapper—if the patron would forgive him for his use of the vernacular.

The patron forgave him.

In that case, Jabez wondered whether he could please have an ash tray, one of decent size?

The patron raised an offended eyebrow. Here, all the ash trays were decent. He snapped his fingers.

A *maître d'hôtel* snapped his fingers. A captain presented an ash tray.

Jabez nodded with approval. "Ah, eighteenth century Sèvres. Eighteenth century, a beautiful century. Sèvres, a beautiful porcelain. An appropriate pyre. You agree?"

The patron, all at once sad again, agreed.

"Pyre?" Zena asked, her lips stiff. "What's—who's going to be burned?"

Jabez reached into his watch pocket and pulled out a card, held it up to Zena.

"This is familiar?" he asked Zena.

Indeed it was.

Jabez lit his gold lighter, held it up to the card.

"One moment!" the patron cried. "You are absolutely determined—?"

"Absolutely."

The patron kissed Jabez first on one cheek, then on the other.

The card did not take easily to burning. It resisted. But Jabez persisted.

When it was all over, when there was nothing but a tiny pearl gray heap of ashes in the tray, Jabez's eyes were very black and his face was very white.

"That does it!" he said. "We are now free."

"Who are we?" Zena asked.

"We are—me. And we are—you. We are now both free."

"Free? I am free?" Zena's eyes darted from Jabez to the patron. "Is this a joke?"

No, it was not a joke they told her in English and in French.

"But why?" Zena could not help asking, "why are

179

you setting me free?"

"Frankly, I do not know. Perhaps it *is* a joke, the whole affair. Perhaps I wished to have the last laugh on your mama. Perhaps I wished to get even. Who knows? After all, tonight you will meet—strangers."

The patron took exception to that. Had Jabez forgotten that here the guest list was gone over with a fine tooth comb? One made of the finest tortoiseshell?

"In any case, tonight the curtain comes down on Jabez." Jabez bowed.

"It was a beautiful play," the patron said. "I will miss you, *mon vieux*, my old friend."

"They will all miss me. One day they will try to replace me with a machine, a computer. As if a machine can do the work of a great artist, create the true illusion. Without me, it won't be the same. I ask you—will the machine exist that can turn the frog into the prince?"

"But no," the patron assured him.

I am free, I am free, Zena repeated over and over again. But what did that mean?

"And now," she heard Jabez say, "the curtain will rise on her."

"Who me?" her voice was very little.

You, they said in English and in French. And from behind potted palms and velvet drapes various people said it in various languages.

"Mademoiselle, here where we do things in the grand manner, for you I had thought first of the *bal masqué*, the masquerade ball, the most beautiful joke of all. But it came to me a better idea. Here for the débuts I have made of the grand ballroom a snow scene from old St. Petersburg, a plantation from your southland, the forest from your woods. There is nothing I have not done for a girl who comes out into society. A girl with a rich papa, you understand. But tonight, I have here the stingiest papa of the season. What do you see here tonight, mademoiselle?" He pointed to the stairway, the landing, the entrance to the ballroom. "Tonight you see nothing. *Rien.* No snowfall. No plantation. *Rien.* Nothing. Not one single flower for his poor little weed of a daughter. But me, *moi-même*, I am famous for the detail, is it not so? *Oui.* So tonight, I, *moi-même*, I make the most beautiful detail of my career. For this party without flowers, I give them one perfect flower—you, mademoiselle, one—"

"Not quite perfect," Jabez interrupted hastily. Before the patron could argue the point, Jabez added, "Take my word for it."

And what if I don't wish to be free? Zena was tempted to ask. What if I refuse? What then?

But the patron, who knew his business, snapped his fingers. A *maître d'hôtel* disappeared into the ballroom; a maid came swiftly from the room *pour les dames.*

"Mademoiselle, you have heard Monsieur Jabez—he has told you that you are now at liberty—"

The maid reaching over to take Zena's cape whispered, "*Vive la liberté!*"

Zena held on to the cape.

"Long live freedom," the patron translated.

Faintly, from behind the closed doors of the ballroom

there was music.

The patron took a dance card out of his pocket, held the pencil poised.

"Mademoiselle, if an old man—" he glanced at Jabez — "who may also retire tonight—may have the honor of the first dance?"

The door to the ballroom was opened; it was a waltz they were playing, still muted but more easily heard. Was it a little Liszt? Or was it a little Chopin?

No matter. One foot tapped.

It would be a waltz; nothing had been overlooked.

The maid took Zena's cape.

One, two, three—One, two, three—

Zena turned to Jabez. His eyes were half closed and he was swaying with the music, conducting with an imaginary baton in his hand.

"Jabez—"

All at once, on an impulse she reached up and kissed Jabez. "*I* will miss you."

Jabez's eyes had flown open and his face was as red as his hair. "No, you won't, not you," he said gruffly. "Now then. One, two, three, one, two, three—" He resumed his conducting.

Floating away in three quarter time, Zena did stop once to look back.

Jabez was leaving; one might even say he was fleeing. But he was not alone. The cat was beside him.

On a settee just outside the ballroom, the debutante's dowager grandmother woke with a start.

"Who is *she?*" she asked, her basset hound eyes watering as they followed Zena.

"I'm afraid I don't know," her frightened companion, who was paid to know such things, whispered. "But, oh madam, the look in her eyes . . . we have never seen anything like it . . . and so green . . . the most beautiful green. . . ."

"I thought we were supposed to have seen everything. Why haven't we seen it before?"

"I don't know, madam, I don't know."

"Well, neither do I. No one knows anything anymore."

The dowager grandmother went back to sleep, and, with her eyes on the ballroom, the companion began to dream.

Inside the ballroom, streaking across its ivory and rose and aquamarine, there was a swirl of green chiffon. Seeing it, the orchestra sent the music swelling up to the vaulted ceiling and around the giant crystal chandelier.

Green chiffon when it is waltzing looks like sea foam. A stag line when it is converging on green chiffon looks like a stag line.

And then.

And then from the dark shadows beyond the dance floor, he came. To be sure, he was not wearing the sweater with the H inside out, but neither was he wearing white tie and tails, nor a dinner jacket—just an ordinary sack suit.

"Who is he?" everyone asked.

Knowing himself exactly who he was, he paid no attention. He tapped a shoulder and then it was he who went whirling off with the girl with the yellow hair. He waltzed her to the farthest edge of the dance floor. And then he waltzed her right off it and, holding her hand, he ran away with her.

"Ah-h-h!" the stag line sighed as the music swelled to a final crescendo.

The boat was just about to leave the slip. But when the captain saw the laughing girl and the laughing young man racing for it, he ordered the engines reversed.

They went to the top deck. All the stars were out that night, and there was a new moon. The skyline of the city never looked better.

As the boat pulled out for its ride across the bay from Manhattan to Staten Island, a stately white ship, heading for the open sea and Europe, saluted the yellow-haired girl and the young man with the crest of a kingfisher by blowing its whistle.

On that ship, there were many girls off to Europe in search of a prince. "Bon Voyage," Zena called out to them. "And good luck." With her free hand, the one that was not holding the young man's, she waved. Herself, she had no need to go to Europe, she thought, as she looked up at the young man.

"And, as for you, you were the one who was not knightable," Zena murmured, "not back there then, not now—"

"Not ever," the young man said firmly. "And now do you know why?"

The answer, it seemed, had been waiting all the time. She did not want this young man changed; this young man was right just the way he was.

In the moonlight, the bay was the color of adventure on high seas.

In those days, the ride on the Staten Island ferry was a trip famous for being romantic. It was a trip that transported you elsewhere, wherever you longed to go. And all for a nickel—and some imagination.

J
CRA

Crayder, Dorothy

The pluperfect of
love

DATE		
FEB 17 1987		